PREFACE

THE sentence from Montaigne, which faces the title-page of this little book, indicates its scope and purpose.

It is based upon studies in the philosophy of folk-tales, in the course of which a large number of examples of curious beliefs and customs bearing on the main incident in certain groups have been collected. Some of these are now 'shuffled up together' round an old Suffolk tale, whose vivacity and humour secure it the first place among the 'Rumpelstiltskin' variants with which it is classed.

Those who have had experience in the gathering of materials illustrative of the several departments of barbaric culture will appreciate the difficulty which has been felt in making selections that suffice to interpret the central idea without obscuring it by a multiplicity of examples. If the book, which is designed mainly for popular reading, therefore makes no pretence to exhaustiveness, it may perhaps have the virtue of being less tedious.

E.C.

Rosemont, 19 Carleton Road,
Tufnell Park N., April 1898

INTRODUCTION

IN commenting on the prominent example of the conversion of the old epics into allegories which is supplied by Tennyson's *Idylls of the King*, whereby the legends 'lose their dream reality without gaining the reality of ordinary life,' Mr. Leslie Stephen remarks that 'as soon as the genuine inhabitants of Fairyland can be interpreted as three virtues or three graces, they cease to fascinate' him. With that confession most people will agree. For alike to those who told the story, and to their hearers, these 'inhabitants of Fairyland' were no buckram-clad personifications of Moralities like the characters in the Mystery Plays of four centuries ago. They were real dwellers in a real Wonderland, whose limits are only those of the broad, deep convert them into vehicles of edification is not merely to empty them of their primitive significance, but to make vain the attempt to understand the conditions which gave birth and long renown to saga and fireside tale. In the dim past when these were woven out of old traditions, no sharp lines severed nature from super-nature; troll and fairy were part of the vagaries which seemed to make up the sum of things at whose core it entered not the mind of man to conceive that unbroken order might be found. Their old mythologies, full of crude and coarse detail, were no fables to the ancient Greeks slowly rising above the barbaric level of ancestors on a plane with the Gold Coast savage who believes his medicine-man when, handing on the traditional cosmogony of the tribe, he tells how the world was made by a big spider. The healthy natured child, who in many things represents the savage stage of thinking, listens without question to the stories of the Giant who hid his heart in a duck's egg on an island out of harm's way, as he vainly hoped; and of Beauty and the Beast, where the princess's curiosity led to the retransformation of the enchanted prince to the shape of loathly monster.

To the secular arm, therefore, be delivered any and every book which, catering for the youngsters, throttles the life of the old folk-tales with coils of explanatory notes, and heaps on their maimed corpses the dead weight of bibliographical appendices. Nevertheless, that which delighted our childhood may instruct our manhood; and notes, appendices, and all the gear of didactic exposition, have their place elsewhere in helping the student, anxious to reach the seed of fact which is covered by the pulp of fiction. For, to effect this is to make approach to man's thoughts and conceptions of himself and his surroundings, to his way of looking at things, and to explanation of his conduct both in work and play. Hence the folk-tale and the game are alike pressed into the service of study of the human mind. Turn where we may, the pastimes of children are seen to mimic the serious pursuits of men. Their dances and romps, their tin soldiers, guns, and trumpets, the dolls and other apparatus of the nursery, and the strategic combats of the playground, have a high antiquity. The game of 'Buck, buck, how many fingers do I hold up?' was played in the streets of Imperial Rome. The ancient Greek 'ostrakinda,' or 'game of the shell,' has its counterpart in one played among the Navajoes of New Mexico. 'Hot cockles' is depicted on Egyptian wall-paintings, and a wooden toy-bird with wheels under its wings, found in the Faym cemetery, is identical with specimens in use among Yakut and Aino children. The players of 'All Round the Mulberry Tree' probably represent a dance of old round a sacred bush; 'Green Gravel' and 'Jenny Jones' are funeral games; 'Forfeits' are relics of divination; and 'Cat's Cradle' belongs to the string puzzles which are played all the world over by savage and civilised.

Whether game and story embody serious elements, or are the outcome of lighter moods, it is this trivial or earnest purpose that we strive to reach. And, notably in the analysis of tales, that effort has been well justified in bringing us, often when least suspected, near some deposit of early thought, near some guesses at a philosophy which embraces all life in a common origin and destiny; and in putting us into touch with instinctive feelings of the Un-cultured mind whose validity has been proved by reason and experience.

A superficial acquaintance with folk-tales reveals the fact that many of them are capable of division into a series of well-marked groups united by a common *motif*, round which imagination has played, 'truth' being thus 'embodied in a tale.' And the interest in this cardinal feature is the greater if it can be shown to contain some primitive philosophy of things which 'has expressed itself in beliefs that have ruled man's conduct, and in rites and ceremonies which are the 'outward and visible signs' of the beliefs. Several groups answer to this requirement. One of them centres round the tale, referred to above, of 'the Giant who had no Heart in his Body,' variants of which have been found from India to the Highlands, and from the Arctic seaboard to Africa. The fundamental idea in this group is the widespread barbaric belief in the separateness of the soul or heart or strength, or whatever else is denominated the seat of life, from the body, whose fate is nevertheless bound up with that of the soul. In the Norse example, a princess wooed by a giant wheedles him, in Delilah--like fashion, into making known in what secret place his heart is hidden. lie tells her that it is in an egg in a duck swimming in a well in a church on an island, all which she straightway repeats to her true love who has stolen into the castle to rescue her. With the aid of a number of helpful animals, a common feature of folk-tales, the lover gets the egg, and as he squeezes it the giant bursts to pieces. Fantastic as all this seems, it is only the accretion of varying detail round a serious belief of which living examples are found throughout the world. Obviously that belief lies at the base of the argument by which Herbert Spencer, Tylor, and others of their school show how theories of the soul and future life were elaborated from barbaric conceptions of the 'other self' which quitted the body for a time in sleep and dreams and swoons, leaving it at death to. return no more, although fitfully visiting its old haunts to help or harm the living. But more than bare hint on these matters lies beyond the purpose of this reference, which is designed to make easier the passage to the significance of the central idea of another group of folk-tales, the masterpiece among which gives its title to this volume.

TOM TIT TOT

THE writer's interest in that group was awakened some years ago when looking over a bundle of old numbers of the Ipswich Journal, in which some odds and ends of local 'notes and queries' were collected. Among these was the story of 'Tom Tit Tot,' which, with another story, 'Cap o' R.ushes' (in this the King Lear incident of testing the love of the three daughters is the *motif*) had been sent to Mr. Hindes Groome, the editor of the 'notes and queries' column, by a lady to whom they had been told in her girlhood by an old West Suffolk nurse. Much of their value lies in their being almost certainly derived from oral transmission through uncultured peasants. The story of 'Tom Tit Tot,' given in the racy dialect of East Anglia, is as follows:--

Well, once upon a time there were a woman and she baked five pies. And when they come out of the oven, they was that overbaked, the crust were too hard to eat. So she says to her darter--

'Maw'r,' says she, 'put you them there pies on the shelf an' leave 'em there a little, an' they'll come agin'--she meant, you know, the crust 'ud get soft.

But the gal, she says to herself, 'Well, if they'll come agin, I'll ate 'em now.' And she set to work and ate 'em all, first and last.

Well, come supper time the woman she said, 'Goo you and git one o' them there pies. I dare say they 'ye came agin now.'

The gal she went an' she looked, and there warn't nothin' but the dishes. So back she come and says she, 'Noo, they ain't come agin.'

'Not none on 'em?' says the mother.

'Not none on 'em,' says she.

'Well, come agin, or not come agin,' says the woman, 'I'll ha' one for supper.'

'But you can't, if they ain't come,' says the gal. 'But I can,' says she. 'Goo you and bring the best of 'em.'

'Best or worst,' says the gal, 'I 'ye ate 'em all, and you can't ha' one till that 's come agin.'

Well, the woman she were wholly bate, and she took her spinnin' to the door to spin, and as she span she sang--

'My darter ha' ate five, five pies to-day--
My darter ha' ate five, five pies to-day.'

The king he were a comin' down the street an he hard her sing, but what she sang he couldn't hare, so he stopped and said--

'What were that you was a singun of, maw'r?'

The woman, she were ashamed to let him hare what her darter had been a doin', so she sang, 'stids o' that--

'My darter ha' spun five, five skeins to-day--
My darter ha' spun five, five skeins to-day.'

'S'ars o' mine!' said the king, 'I never heerd tell of any on as could do that.'

Then he said: 'Look you here, I want a wife, and I'll marry your darter. But look you here,' says he, "leven months out o' the year she shall have all the vittles she likes to eat, and all the gownds she likes to git, and all the cumpny she likes to hey; but the last month o' the year she 'll ha' to spin five skeins iv'ry day, an' if she doon't, I shall kill her.'

'All right,' says the woman: for she thowt what a grand marriage that was. And as for them five skeins, when te come tew, there'd be plenty o' ways of gettin' out of it, and likeliest, he 'd ha' forgot about it.

Well, so they was married. An' for 'leven months the gal had all the vittles she liked to ate, and all the gownds she liked to git, an' all the cumpny she liked to hev.

But when the time was gettin' oover, she began to think about them there skeins an' to wonder if he had 'em in mind. But not one word did he say about 'em, an' she whoolly thowt he 'd forgot 'em.

Howsivir, the last day o' the last month, he takes her to a room she'd niver set eyes on afore. There worn't nothin' in it but a spinnin' wheel and a stool. An' says he, 'Now, me dear, hare yow 'll be shut in to-morrow with some vittles and some flax, and if you hairi't spun five skeins by the night, yar hid 'll goo off.'

An' awa' he went about his business.

Well, she were that frightened. She'd allus been such a gatless mawther, that she didn't se much as know how to spin, an' what were she to dew tomorrer, with no one to come nigh her to help her. She sat down on a stool in the kitchen, and lork! how she did cry!

Howsivir, all on a sudden she hard a sort of a knockin' low down on the door. She upped and oped it, an' what should she see but a small little black thing with a long tail. That looked up at her right kewrious, an' that said--

'What are yew a cryin' for?'

'Wha 's that to yew?' says she.

'Niver yew mind,' that said, 'but tell me what you 're a cryin' for.'

'That oon't dew me noo good if I dew,' says she. 'Yew doon't know that,' that said, an' twirled that's tail round.

'Well,' says she, 'that oon't dew no harm, if that doon't dew no good,' and she upped and told about the pies an' the skeins an' everything.

'This is what I'll dew,' says the little black thing:

'I 'll come to yar winder iv'ry mornin' an' take the flax an' bring it spun at night.'

'What 's your pay?' says she.

That looked out o' the corners o' that's eyes an' that said: 'I 'll give you three guesses every night to guess my name, an' if you hain't guessed it afore the month 's up, yew shall be mine.'

Well, she thowt she'd be sure to guess that's name afore the month was up. 'All right,' says she, 'I agree.'

'All right,' that says, an' lork! how that twirled that's tail.

Well, the next day, her husband he took her inter the room, an' there was the flax an' the day's vittles.

'Now, there 's the flax,' says he, 'an' if that ain't spun up this night off goo yar hid.' An' then he went out an' locked the door.

He'd hardly goon, when there was a knockin' agin the winder.

She upped and she oped it, and there sure enough was the little oo'd thing a settin' on the ledge.

'Where's the flax?' says he.

'Here te be,' says she. And she gonned it to him. Well, come the evenin', a knockin' come agin to the winder. She upped an' she oped it, and there were the little oo'd thing, with five skeins of flax on his arm.

'Here te be,' says he, an' he gonned it to her.

'Now, what 's my name?' says he.

'What, is that Bill?' says she.

'Noo, that ain't,' says he. An' he twirled his tail.

'Is that Ned?' says she.

'Noo, that ain't,' says he. An' he twirled his tail.

'Well, is that Mark?' says she.

'Noo, that ain't,' says he. An' he twirled his tail harder, an' awa' he flew.

Well, when har husban' he come in: there was the five skeins riddy for him. 'I see I shorn't hey for to kill you tonight, me dare,' says he. 'Yew 'ii hey yar vittles and yar flax in the mornin',' says he, an' away he goes.

Well, ivery day the flax an' the vittles, they was browt, an' ivery day that there little black impet used for to come monin's and evenin's. An' all the day the mawther she set a tryin' fur to think of names to say to it when te come at night. But she niver hot on the right one. An' as that got to-warts the end o' the month, the impet that began for to look soo maliceful, an' that twirled that's tail faster an' faster each time she gave a guess.

At last te come to the last day but one. The impet that come at night along o' the five skeins, an' that said--

'What, hain't yew got my name yet?'

'Is that Nicodemus?' says she. 'Noo, t'ain't,' that says.

'Is that Sammle?' says she.

'Noo, t'ain't,' that says.

'A-well, is that Methusalem?' says she.

'Noo, t'ain't that norther,' he says. Then that looks at her with that's eyes like a cool o' fire, an' that says, 'Woman, there 's only to-morrer night, an' then yar'll be mine!' n' away te flew.

Well, she felt that horrud. Howsomediver, she hard the king a coming along the passage. In he came, an' when he see the five skeins, he says, says he--

'Well, me dare,' says he, 'I don't see but what yew 'll ha' your skeins ready tomorrer night as well, an' as I reckon I shorn't ha' to kill you, I 'll ha' supper in here to-night.' So they brought supper, an' another stool for him, and down the tew they sat.

Well, he hadn't eat but a mouthful or so, when he stops and begins to laugh.

'What is it?' says she.

'A-why,' says he, 'I was out a-huntin' to-day, an' I got away to a place in the wood I'd never seen afore. An' there was an old chalk pit. An' I heerd a sort of a hummin', kind o'. So I got off my hobby, an' I went right ~quiet to the pit, an' I looked down. Well, what should there be but the funniest little black thing yew iver set eyes on. An' what was that a dewin' on, but that had a little spinnin' wheel, an' that were a spinnin' wonnerful fast, an' a twirlin' that's tail. An' as that span, that sang--

'Nimmy nimmy not,
My name's Tom Tit Tot.'

Well, when the mawther heerd this, she fared as if she could ha' jumped outer her skin for joy, but she di'n't say a word.

Next day, that there little thing looked soo maliceful when he come for the flax. An' when night came, she heerd that a knockin' agin the winder panes. She oped the winder, an' that come right in on the ledge. That were grinnin' from are to are, an' Oo! tha's tail were twirlin' round so fast.

'What's my name?' that says, as that gonned her the skeins.

'Is that Solomon?' she says, pretendin' to be afeard.

'Noo, t'ain't,' that says, an' that come fudder inter the room.

'Well, is that Zebedee?' says she agin.

'Noo, t'ain't,' says the impet. An' then that laughed an' twirled that's tail till yew cou'n't hardly see it.

'Take time, woman,' that says; 'next guess, an' you're mine.' An' that stretched out that's black hands at her.

Well, she backed a step or two, an' she looked at it, and then she laughed out, an' says she, a pointin' of her finger at it--

'Nimmy nimmy not,
Yar name's Tom 'Fit Tot.'

Well when that hard her, that shruck awful an' awa' that flew into the dark, an' she niver saw it noo more.

Variants Of Tom Tit Tot

THERE would be only profitless monotony in printing the full texts, or even in giving abstracts, of the numerous variants of this story which have been collected. A list of these, with such comment as may perchance be useful to a special class of readers, is supplied in the Appendix. Here it suffices to remark that in all of them the plot centres round the discovery of the name of the maleficent actor in the little drama, and to give a summary of a few of the most widely spread stories in which, as might be expected, a certain variety of incident occurs. These are chosen from Scotland, Tyrol, the Basque provinces, and the Far East, the variants from this last containing the fundamental idea in an entirely different plot. To these follow a Welsh variant in which our joy at the defeat of the demon or witch in most of the stories is changed into sorrow for the fairy.

The Scotch 'Whuppity Stooric' tells of a man who 'gaed to a fair ae day,' and was never more heard of. His widow was left with a 'sookin' lad bairn,' and a sow that 'was soon to farra.' Going to the sty one day, she saw, to her distress, the sow ready 'to gi'e up the ghost,' and as she sat down with her bairn and 'grat sairer than ever she did for the loss o' her am goodman,' there came an old woman dressed in green, who asked what she would give her for curing the sow. Then they 'watted thooms' on the bargain, by which the woman promised to give the green fairy anything she liked, and the sow was thereupon made well. To the mother's dismay the fairy then said that she would have the bairn. 'But, said she, 'this I'll let ye to wut, I canna by the law we leeve on take your bairn till the third day after this day; and no' then, if ye can tell me my right name.' For two days the poor woman wandered, 'cuddlin' her bairn,' when, as she came near an old quarry-hole, she heard the 'burring of a lint-wheel, and a voice lilting a song,' and then saw the green fairy at her wheel, 'singing like ony precentor '--

'Little kens our guid dame at hame

That Whuppity Stoorie is my name.'

Speeding home glad-hearted, she awaited the fairy's coming; and, being a 'jokus woman,' pulled a long face, begging that the bairn might be spared and the sow taken, and when this was spurned, offering herself. 'The deil 's in the daft jad,' quo' the fairy, 'wha in a' the earthly wand wad ever meddle wi' the likes o' thee?' Then the woman threw off her mask of grief, and, making 'a curchie down to the ground,' quo' she, 'I might hae had the wit to ken that the likes o' me is na fit to tie the warst shoe-strings o' the heich and mighty princess, Whuppity Stoorie.' 'Gin a fluff o' gunpouder had come out o' the grund, it couldna hae gart the fairy loup heicher nor she did; syne doun she came again, dump on her shoe-heels, and, whurlin' round, she ran down the brae, scraichin' for rage, like a houlet chased wi' the witches.'

11

In the Tyrolese story, a count, while hunting in a forest, is suddenly confronted by a dwarf with fiery red eyes and a beard down to his knees, who rolls his eyes in fury, and tells the count that he must pay for trespassing on the mannikin's territory either with his life or the surrender of his wife. The count pleads for pardon, and the dwarf so far modifies his terms as to agree that if within a month the countess cannot find out his name, she is to be his. Then, escorting the count to the forest bounds where stood an ancient fir-tree, it is bargained that the dwarf will there await the countess, who shall have three guesses three times, nine in all. The month expires, and she then repairs to the rendezvous to make her first round of guesses, giving the names, 'Janne,' 'Fichte,' and 'Fohre.' The dwarf shrieks with merriment over her failure, and when she returns to the castle she enters the chapel and offers earnest prayers for help in guessing the right name. But the next day, when she gives the names 'Hafer,' 'Pleuten,' and 'Turken,' repeats the failure, and calls forth the dwarf's unholy glee. When she comes to the tree on the third day, he is not there. So she wandered from the spot till she reached a lovely valley, and, seeing a tiny house, went on tiptoe, and peeping in at the window heard the dwarf singing his name in a verse as he hopped gaily on the hearth. The countess hurries back to the tree in high spirits, and when the dwarf appears she artfully withholds the secret she has learned till the last chance is hers. 'Pur,' she guesses, and the dwarf chortles; 'Ziege,'t then he bounds in the air; 'Purzinigele,' she shouts derisively, and then the dwarf rolling his red eyes in rage, doubles his fist, and disappears for ever in the darkness.

In Basque folk-tale, a mother is beating her lazy girl, when the lord of a castle hard by, who is passing at the time, asks what all the pother is about, and is told that the girl's beauty makes her saucy and indolent. Then follow the usual incidents, with the exception that a witch, instead of a demon, comes to aid the girl, to whom the lord then offers marriage if she can get a certain amount of work done within a given time, the witch's bargain being that the girl must remember her name, Marie Kirikitoun, a year and a day hence. The wedding takes place, and as the year end draws near, sadness falls on the bride, despite the holding of grand festivals to gladden her spirits. For she had forgotten the witch's name. At one of the feastings an old woman knocks at the door, and when a servant tells her that all the high jinks are kept up to make her mistress cheerful, the beldame says that if the lady had seen what she had seen, her laughter would run free enough. So the servant bids her come in, and then she tells how she had seen an old witch leaping and bounding from one ditch to another, and singing all the time, 'Houpa, houpa, Marie Kirikitoun, nobody will remember my name.' Whereupon the bride became merry-hearted, rewarded the old woman, and told the enraged witch her name when she came for fulfilment of the bargain.

In *Sagas from the Far East*, a king sends his son on travel that he may gain all kinds of knowledge. The prince takes, as his favourite companion, the son of the prime minister, who, on their return journey, burning with envy at the superior wisdom of his royal comrade, entices him into a forest and kills him. As the prince dies, he utters the word,

'Abaraschika.' When the murderer reaches the palace, he tells the sorrowing king how the prince fell sick unto death, and that he had time to speak only the above word. Thereupon the king summoned his seers and magicians, and threatened them with death if they did not, within seven days, interpret the meaning of 'Abaraschika.' That time had well-nigh expired when a student came beckoning to them, bidding them not despair, for, while sleeping beneath a tree, he had heard a bird telling his young ones not to cry for food, since the Khan would slay a thousand men on the morrow because they could not find out the meaning of 'Abaraschika.' And the meaning, said the bird, was this:--'My bosom friend hath enticed me into a thick grove, and hath taken away my life.' So the seers and magicians hastened to report what they had heard to the king, who thereupon put the murderer to death.

The Welsh story (one of several closely allied in detail) tells that once upon a Lime the youthful heir of Ystrad, on adventure bent, wandered by the banks of the Gwyrfai stream that issues from Quellyn's lake. As night fell he hid him. self by a bush near the spot where the 'Tywyth Teg,' or 'Fair Family' (the 'Folk of the Re~ Coat'), held their revels. The moon shone in r cloudless sky, and the youth had not long to wait before he saw the 'little people' trool forth to the dance. Among these was one who straightway kindled his love, for never mort graceful maiden or light-footed dancer had h seen. The longer he watched her, the hotter grew his desire, till, making resolve to seize her, he 'sprang like a lion into the middle of the circle' just when the fairies were most enjoying the swing of the dance, and carried her off in his arms to Ystrad. 'Her companions vanished like a breath in July as they heard the shrill voice of their sister crying for help.' When the youth reached home he strove by every gentle art in his power to make the fairy happy, and she served him well in return, being obdurate only in one thing. 'He could in nowise prevail on her to tell him her name,' and vain were all his efforts to discover it, till one evening, as he was driving two of his cows to the meadow, he came again to the spot where he had captured the fairy. He hid himself, as before, in the thicket, and when the troop of the Red-coated appeared, he heard them saying to one another that when they last came thither a mortal had carried off their sister Penelope. Glad-hearted, the youth hurried' home and called the fairy by her name, whereupon grief clouded her face. Her beauty and distress moved him the more to urge that she who had been his faithful serving-maid would become his wife; and although she long refused him, she at last consented, but only on his promising that if ever he struck her with iron she should be free to leave him. For years he kept his word, but, one day, as they went together to catch a wild horse in the field, he threw the bridle at him, and by mischance struck his fairy wife with the iron bit, whereupon she straightway vanished.

HERE we may interpose a brief example from the Welsh group, as bearing on the origin of the alliterative name 'Tom Tit Tot.'

A farmer's wife at Llanlestin often lent her gradell and padell (the flat iron on which the dough is put for baking, and the pan which is put over it) to a fairy, who, on returning the articles, always brought a loaf of bread in acknowledgment. One day she begged the loan of a troell-bach, or spinning-wheel, whereupon the woman asked her name, which the fairy refused to tell. So she was tracked and watched at her spinning, when she was heard singing to the whirr of the wheel =

'Little does she know
That Trwtyn-Tratyn
Is my name.'

In an Irish variant, to which reference occurs in Taylor's translation of Grimm's *Rumpelstiltskin*, the fairy sings--

'Little does my lady wot
That my name is Trit a Trot.'

As 'Trwtyn-Tratyn' is not Welsh, there remains for the curious the search after the original source and mode of transmission of the Suffolk tale. That question is obviously bound up with the general subject of the origin and migration of stories, a question to which no answer is likely to be forthcoming in the absence of documents. In some quarters high hopes were indulged that the ingathering of the variants of one group of stories, and the framing of charts of its geographical distribution, would enable us to trace the parent type to its original home. Cinderella' was chosen, and by the application of great labour, illumined by scholarship, Miss Roalfe Cox prepared three hundred and forty-five abstracts of as many versions of that familiar ale, adding tables of areas in which they are found. The result of all the toil and talent thus employed was to leave the question exactly where we found it. In Mr. Andrew Lang's words: 'There is not a sign of her birth-country on Cinderella; not a mark to show that she came from India, or Babylonia, or Egypt, or any other old cradle of civilisation.'

That a large number of stories have originated in definite centres, and have been carried from place to place, 'goes without saying.' Racial intercourse was already active in the later Neolithic age, and East gave to West of its intellectual, as well as of its material, products. 'Folk-tales might well be scattered abroad in the same manner by merchantmen gossiping over their Khan fires, by Sidonian mariners chatting in the sounding *loggia* of an Homeric house, by the slave dragged from his home and passed from owner to owner across Africa or Europe, by the wife who, according to primitive law, had to be chosen from an alien clan.' There is weight, also, in Mr. Hindes Groome's arguments on behalf of those ubiquitous nomads, the gypsies, who, especially in past times, had every facility for diffusing their stories among all conditions of men. On the other hand, the fundamental idea at the core of certain stories is explained by the fact that at corresponding levels of culture the human mind accounts for the same things in much the same way. Ideas are universal; incidents are local. For example, the conceptions of a united heaven and earth forced asunder by some defiant hero so that light may be given to the children of men, and of a sky-piercing tree whereby heaven can be reached, have given rise to myths and folk-tales 'from China to Peru.'

All that we can say by way of approach to the solution of a question whose settlement would throw light on intercourse between peoples, is that where coincidences in stories extend to minute detail, a common origin may be assumed, but that where only a like idea is present as the chief *motif* without correspondences in incidental details, independent origin is probable. Strabosays that 'in the childhood of the world men, like children, had to be taught by tales'; and, certainly, their invention is the monopoly of no one race.

ALTHOUGH the selection of only a few of the numerous variants of 'Tom Tit Tot' relieves us from comment on sundry differences in detail between the whole of them, there are points of interest which call for notice before we advance to the central idea of the story. Some are of little moment, as where, in the Lorraine variant, the devil's age, instead of his name, has to be guessed to secure quittance from the bargain. Others,. as in the example of the helpful bird in the Eastern story, would carry us into the wide, and fascinating subject of barbaric belief in community between man and all living things beneath him. Of the remainder, three claim comment--the superstitions about iron, the incidents of spinning, and of outwitting the demon or other maliceful agent.

(a) SUPERSTITIONS ABOUT IRON

The reference to iron is one among other examples of incidental features in folk-tales which not only evidence their antiquity, but throw light on the customs and beliefs embodied in them, which otherwise would remain obscure. The unlettered are conservative, both from fear and the power of tradition. The devil may have been 'the first Whig,' which, nowadays, would spell Radical, but whoever, whether man or fiend, challenged authority to produce its credentials, has that distinction. Things new or unusual, being unknown, are objects of dread in the degree that mystery invests them; and this explains, among other matters, the old ideas which attached to iron, and the retention of stone instruments for sacred rites and ceremonies, as, for example, of flint knives, in mummy-incision, among the ancient Egyptians; and among the Jews in circumcision; of obsidian or other stone sacrificial knives among the Mexicans; while in Scotland, in making the *clavie*, a kind of Yuletide fire-wheel, a stone hammer was used. Witches and fairies are creations of the Stone Age; the peasant-folk see in the delicately shaped flint arrow-heads of our Neolithic forerunners the 'elf-darts' wherewith the 'good people' maim men and cattle. And the dread with which these creatures are believed to regard iron explains its widespread use as a charm against them. Old Aubrey says that 'a Horse-shoe nailed on the threshold of the dore is yet in fashion, and nowhere more than in London. It ought (Mr. Lilly says) to be a Horse-shoe that one finds by chance on the road. The end of it is to prevent the power of witches that come into your house. So in Germany the common people doe naile such an Horse-shoe on the threshold of the doore. So neere the mainmast in ships' As many a stable-door and mainmast testify, the nailing of horse-shoes to 'keep off the pixies,' and, conversely, to bring luck to farmer and sailor, thrives to this day. The magical power of iron is shown in the hero-legends wherein, for

16

example, King Arthur's wonder-working sword Excalibur plays part, while homelier illustrations are given in the use of iron tongs or scissors to protect a new-born babe from being stolen by the fairies. Among the Kols of India, when a child is born, the umbilical cord is cut and buried in the room, and over it a fire is lit in an earthen pot, into which a bit of iron is put, as a protection against evil spirits who may assail mother or infant In county Donegal, when churning is started, the tongs are put in the fire, or a piece of heated iron is put under the chum, and kept there till the work is finished. The Hindus consider it unlucky to visit the sick at night, lest some prowling demon follow the visitor and then haunt the invalid. But if a piece of iron be taken, the demon thinks that his hair may be cut therewith, whereby he becomes enslaved; so he keeps clear. The name of the metal is itself an effective charm. In Arab belief the zdba'ah or sand-whirlwind, which sweeps, pillar-like, across the land, is due to the flight of a jinnee, and therefore, when its approach is seen, one of the charms uttered is, 'Iron, thou unlucky,' because the very name is believed to drive the jinn away. The aborigines of Victoria thought that dust-storms were due to Kootchee, the Australian evil spirit, and the more daring among them would throw boomerangs at these blinding whirlwinds.

(b) WOMAN AS SPINSTER AND FARMER

Wellnigh all the heroines in the 'Tom Tit Tot' group are set the task of spinning, in a magic space of time, a large quantity of flax, or, as in the Swedish variant, the still harder task of spinning straw into gold, and so forth. Prominence is therefore given to the wheel and distaff as woman's typical occupation. The old and now discredited school of interpreters, represented in this country chiefly by Professor Max Muller and Sir George W. Cox, which resolved every myth and folk-tale, and occasionally even history itself, into solar elements, explains the spinning incident as the dawn-maiden, be she Penelope or the miller's daughter, weaving 'her robe of clouds.' But a more sober school of interpretation is, like wisdom, 'justified of its children.' That was a relatively advanced stage in human progress 'when Adam delved and Eve span,' because among barbaric people the woman does both. War and the chase fill the lives of men; and the work of handling both spade and spindle falls to the women. They were the first agriculturists, and over a wide area of the arable earth they still 'hold the field.' While the man was fighting or chasing the coveted game, the woman was grubbing up roots and pounding seeds or nuts to keep hunger from the hut, round whose clearing she learned to sow the cereal and plant the fruit-tree. In East Africa she tills the soil, tends the cattle, and does the bartering; among the Niam-Niam the men devote themselves to hunting, and leave the cultivation of the soil to the women, who, among the Monbuttoo, do all the husbandry from hoeing to harvest. Herodotus (Book iv. 6) says of the Thracians that 'they accounted idleness as the most honourable thing, and to be a tiller of the ground the most dishonourable.' Among the ancient Peruvians, farm-work fell entirely to the womenfolk, while the rudest form of agriculture is found among the squaws of Central California, who use their fingers as hoes, rubbing the earth to powder between their hands. In modern Palestine, although the men do the ploughing, the women follow to drop the seed into the furrows; and in the Sonneberg district, in Germany, and indeed throughout Europe, the preparation, planting, and sowing, the harvesting and thrashing, are largely done by women. It is, therefore, an error to speak of fieldwork by woman as a sign of her degradation; for wherever it now exists, although often evidencing man's laziness or brutality, it is a survival of primitive conditions when everything domestic devolved on the female. Among the indoor duties were the keeping of the hearth and weaving. With the long grass as primitive broom, woman tidied the house, and with the primitive spindle-stick she twisted the plant-fibres into yarn. The stone spindle-whorls found among other relics of early Neolithic deposits witness to the high antiquity of an art which ultimately became, both in symbol and language, the type of womans work. How much this all bears on her long foremost place in social organisation, lies beyond our province to deal with. But, as related to what follows, it must be borne in mind that the roots of social unity lie in blood-relationship between mother and offspring rather than between father and offspring. For in the unsettled conditions of barbaric life, when intercourse between the sexes was irregular--the absence or fitful movements of the men leaving the care of home and children to the women,--he was a wise father who knew his own child. Birth and the early nourishment of offspring were the great factors, and hence not only arose the tie of blood-relationship through the mother. but the tracing of descent along the female line both being grouped under what is known as 'mother-right.' Thus, to quote from an able essay by Mr. Karl Pearson on a subject which was originally dealt with some years ago by Bachofen, MacLennan, and other students o~ ancient social groups, 'the mother would be at least the nominal head of the family, the bearer of its traditions, its knowledge, and its religion. Hence we should expect to find that the deities of a mother-right group were female, and that the primitive goddesses were accompanied, not by husband, but by child or brother. The husband and father being insignificant or entirely absent, there would thus easily arise myths of virgin and child, and brother and sister, deities. The goddess of the group would naturally be served by a priestess rather than by a priest. The woman, as depository of family custom and tribal lore, the wise woman, the sibyl, the witch, would hand down to her daughters the knowledge of the religious observances, of the power of herbs, the mother-lore in the mother-tongue, possibly also in some form of symbol or rune, such as a priestly caste love to enshroud their mysteries in. The symbols of these goddesses would be the symbols of woman's work and woman's civilisation,--the distaff, the pitchfork, and the broom, not the spear, the axe, and the hammer.' Herein lies the key to the femininity of the larger number of corn and vegetable and spinning deities, whether one or triune, 'the divine mothers who travel round and visit houses, from whom mankind learned the occupations and arts of housekeeping and husbandry, spinning, weaving, tending the hearth, sowing and reaping.' Ceres, eat whose nod the wheat-field shakes,' to whom the corn-thief, by the code of the Twelve Tables, was hanged as an offering; Persephone, whom Demeter seeks sorrowing, to find her with the upsprouting corn; Xilomen, the Mexican maize-goddess; Nirdu, among the Teutons,--one and all subordinate to the mighty food-giving Earth-mother, known by many names, Erda, Demeter, Pachamama, Dharitri, but everywhere worshipped as the giver of life, whose motherhood, as among the aboriginal Americans, was no mere figure of speech, but an article of positive belief. Naming among hearth-goddesses only the Roman Vesta, the Greek Hestia, and the Teutonic Hiodyn, our more immediate interest in this digression centres round the spinning deities and wise women. The Greeks put spindle and distaff in the hands of several of their goddesses, as of Artemis, Leto, and Athène, the last-named recalling to mind the legend of Arachne's challenge to the goddess to compete with her in the art of weaving. When Arachne produced the cloth on which the loves of the gods were depicted, Athène, enraged at finding no fault in it, tore the work to pieces, whereupon the despairing Arachne hanged herself. But Athène loosened the rope and changed it into a cobweb, Arachne becoming a spider. With the Greek Fates, of whom, according to Hesiod, Clotho spins the web of man's destiny, while Lachesis allots and Atropos cuts the thread, may be compared the weaving of Helgi's fate by the three Norns of Teutonic myth. Stretching the golden cord across the heaven, one Norn hid an end of the thread eastward, another Norn hid an end westward, while a third fastened it northward, the region between the eastern and western ends falling to Helgi's share. The hieroglyph of the great Egyptian goddess Neith was a shuttle, but she lies too remote for knowledge of the degree in which she was a spinning deity. Not so our western Berchtá and Holda, round whom, and their degraded forms in witches, many a legend clusters. To Holda is assigned the cultivation of flax. She gives spindles to industrious girls, and spins their reels full for them overnight, but she burns or spoils the distaffs of lazy maidens. 'On her coming at Christmas, all the distaffs are well stocked, and left standing for her; by Carnival, when she turns homeward, all the spinning must be finished, and the staffs kept out of her sight, otherwise her curse is on the disobedient. The concealment of the implements shows the sacredness of her holy day as a time of rest; an idea transferred, like many others, to the Virgin Mary, on whose holy days spinning is forbidden. Berchta spoils whatever spinning she finds unfinished the last day of the year, and, 'in the North, from Yule day to New Year's day, neither wheel nor windlass must go round.' In Thuringen, songs rose to Frau Holle as the women dressed the flax; and in Lower Austria, Walpurg (whence the name of the great witchgathering, Walpurgisnacht) goes round the fields at harvest-time with a spindle to bless them. In Bavaria, 'flax will not thrive unless it is sown by women, and this has to be done with strange ceremonies, including the scattering over the field of the ashes of a fire made of wood consecrated during matins. As high as the maids jump over the fires on the hilltops on Midsummer Night, so high will the flax grow; but we find also that as high as the bride springs from the table on her marriage night, so high will the flax grow in that year.

19

In Sweden no spinning is done on Thursday night, for fear of offending the spirit who watches over the cattle and the crops. The twisting of the thread and the downward pull of the spindle might affect the growth of the corn. With which examples of ' sympathetic magic' we may couple that given by Mr. Frazer. 'In the interior of Sumatra the rice is sown by women who, in sowing, let their hair hang loose down their back, in order that the rice may grow luxuriantly and have long stalks.' The day after Twelfth Day was called St. Distaff's Day, when spinning was resumed, as in Herrick's lines -

'Partly work and partly play,
Ye must on St. Distaffe's day;
If the maids a-spinning go,
Burn the flax and fire the tow;
Give St. Distaffe all the right,
Then bid Christmas sport good night.'

At Pergine in Tyrol, within recent years, the friend of the bridegroom carried a spinning-wheel, with flax wound round the distaff, in the wedding procession.

In these illustrations of the prominence given to spinning in popular belief and ritual, no line has been drawn between the part severally played by goddess and by witch. Earth supplies the pattern of heavenly things, and therefore the gods and goddesses, with the swarm of godlings, are for the most part mortals variously magnified, whose deeds are the rejection of those which fill the life of man. As for the witch, she may be regarded as the degraded and demon-inspired representative of the priestess and medicine-woman, who still survive in barbaric communities. Weatherwise, as all folk become who, with anxious outlook on the harvest of both land and sea, watch the skies; skilled in the virtue of simples through testing of the qualities of plants; wielder of the pitchfork, the broom, and the distaff, tamer of the cat, as, in his more adventurous life, man was tamer of the wolf, making the devourer of the flock to be the guardian of the fold,--here are the elements out of which was shaped the monstrous nightmare that terrorised mankind and sent thousands to the gallows or the stake.

(c) THE GULLIBLE DEVIL

The stories of the gullibility of the devil are incidents in the history of his decline and fall. Ridicule paved the way to a doom which comparative mythology, in explaining him, has sealed. The ridicule followed his defeat in his own realm of trickery and cunning by mortals. It was a sincere belief among Scotch theologians of the seventeenth century that his cunning so increased with age that he became more than a match for the cleverest.

20

Abercromby, in his *Physick of the Soule*, speaks of the devil 'as now almost of six thousand years, and of great wilyness and experience.' But man is a combative animal, and the feeling that the devil was ever on the watch to trip him up or outwit him, warmed rather than chilled his fighting instinct. In the belief that the devil's favourite method was the bargaining for both body and soul, that he might win both. the spirit of rivalry in the game of huckstering was aroused, so that it became a contest of 'pull devil, pull baker,' as the saying goes. As the old legends show, and as is also manifest in the 'Tom Tit Tot' group of stories, he is the transformed giant or wizard with the superadded features of the fiend whose aim it is to induce the unwary to agree to sell themselves to him at the price of some fleeting advantage. Hence, when he is checkmated, great is the joy at the discomfiture of the 'stupid beast,' as Pope Gregory the Great called him. And of this defeat many a legend tells. In northern saga, King Olaf desired to build a church greater than any yet seen, but lacked the means to accomplish this. As he walked 'twixt hill and dale he met a troll, who, when he heard the king's wish, offered to build the church for him within a given time, stipulating that he was to have the sun and moon, or Olaf himself, in payment. The king agreed; the church was to be large enough to allow seven priests to preach in it at the same time without disturbing one another, and ere long the structure was finished, except the roof and spire. Perplexed at the bargain which he had made, Olaf once more wandered over hill and dale, when suddenly he heard a child cry from within a mountain, while a giantess quieted it with these words, 'Hush, hush, to-morrow comes thy father, Wind and Weather, home, bringing both sun and moon, or saintly Olaf's self.' Overjoyed at this discovery, the king turned home, arriving just in time to see the spire being fixed. He cried out, 'Wind and Weather, thou hast set the spire askew,' when instantly the giant fell off the ridge of the roof with a fearful crash, and burst into a thousand pieces, which were nothing but flint stones. In Swedish legend a giant promises to build a church for the White Christ, if Laurentius can find out his name, otherwise he must forfeit his eyes. As in the Olaf story, the giantess is overheard hushing her crying child and uttering the giant's name.

In the great collection of Welsh manuscripts published by Owen Jones in the beginning of this century, the story of the battle of Achren precedes some verses. It was fought on account of a white roebuck and a puppy which were of Hades. Amathaon, son of Don, had caught them. Therefore he fought with Arawn, King of Hades, and there was in the engagement on the side of Hades a man who could not be vanquished unless his name could be discovered; while there was a woman on the other side called Achren, whose name was to be found out before her side could be vanquished. Gwydion, son of Don, guessed the man's name, and sang the two following englyns. They are the verses alluded to, and they embody Gwydion's guess as to the man's name, which he discovered to be Bran; and as Bran, which means a 'crow,' is one of the appellations of the terrene god, he may be supposed to have been a principal in the fight, that is to say, he was probably the King of Hades himself. Cognate with the foregoing legend of the discomfiture of the devil is that which tells how he agrees to build a house for a peasant at the price of the man's soul, the contract to be null and void if the work is not finished before cockcrow.

Just as day dawns, and as the devil is putting on the last tile, the peasant wakens up all the roosters by imitating their crowing. Or the devil helps to construct a bridge on condition that he receives in payment the soul of the first thing that crosses it, and while he is on the watch to seize his prize, a chamois or dog rushes past him. In the well-known story of the shadowless man, the devil agrees to take the hindmost in a race, and is able to grasp only the shadow of the rearmost runner. The fiend is also befooled by one man, who whistles the Gospel which he has bound himself not to say, and by the refusal of another to carry out his bargain at the fall of the leaf because the foliage sculptured on the church columns is still on the boughs. In the venerable street play of ' Punch and Judy' the climax is reached when, after shamming defeat by the devil, Punch seizes him and strings him to the gallows. The story is told of some angry lookers-on stoning a showman who reversed the traditions of the play by letting the devil carry off Punch. These examples, of which a store may be gathered from Grimm, Thorpe, and other collectors, fall into line with the typical incident of the befooling and discomfiture of the demon in one shape or sex and another in 'Tom Tit Tot' and his variants, along the main track of which group of folk-tales we may now advance without further digression.

BARBARIC IDEAS ABOUT NAMES

BEFORE the discovery of iron; before the invention of the art of spinning; before the formulation of the theory of spirits, against whose wiles mortals might successfully plot,--men had found the necessity of inventing signs or symbols wherewith to distinguish one another. Among these was the choice of personal names, and it is in this that the justification exists for assuming the name-incident in 'Tom Tit Tot' to be probably the most archaic element in the story. Barbaric man believes that his name is a vital part of himself, and therefore that the names of other men and of superhuman beings are also vital parts of themselves. He further believes that to know the name is to put its owner, whether he be deity, ghost, r mortal, in the power of another, involving risk of harm or destruction to the named. He therefore takes all kinds of precautions to conceal his name, often from his friend, and always from his foe.

This belief, and the resulting acts, as will be shown presently, are a part of that general confusion between the objective and the subjective--in other words, between names and things or between symbols and realities--which is a universal feature of barbaric modes of thought. This confusion attributes the qualities of living things to things not living; it lies at the root of all fetishism and idolatry; of all witchcraft, shamanism, and other instruments which are as keys to the invisible kingdom of the dreaded.

Where such ideas prevail, everything becomes a vehicle of magic, and magic, be it remembered, rules the life of the savage. It is, as Adolf Bastian aptly remarks, 'the physics of mankind in a state of nature,' because in the perception, however blurred or dim, of some relation between things, science is born. To look for any consistency in barbaric philosophy is to disqualify ourselves for understanding it, and the theories of it which aim at symmetry are their own condemnation. Yet that philosophy, within its own irregular confines, works not illogically. Ignorant of the properties of things, but ruled by the superficial likenesses which many exhibit, the barbaric mind regards them as vehicles of good or evil, chiefly evil, because things are feared in the degree that they are unknown, and because, where life is mainly struggle, man is ever on the watch against malice-working agencies, wizards, medicine-men, and all their kin. That he should envisage the intangible--that his name should be an entity, an integral part of himself, may the less surprise us when it is remembered that language, from the simple phrases of common life to the highest abstract terms, rests on the concrete.

To 'apprehend' a thing is to 'seize' or 'lay hold' of it; to 'possess' a thing is to 'sit by' or 'beset' it. To call one man a 'sycophant' is to borrow the term 'fig-blabber,' applied by the Greeks to the informer against those who broke the Attic law prohibiting the export of figs; to call another man 'supercilious' is to speak of him as 'raising his eyebrows'; while, as we all know, the terms 'disaster' and 'lunatic' preserve the old belief in the influence of the heavenly bodies on human life. Even the substantive verb 'to be,' the 'most bodiless and colourless of all our words,' is made up of the relics of several verbs which once had a distinct physical significance. 'Be' contained the idea of 'growing'; 'am, art, is,' and 'are,' the idea of 'sitting'; 'was' and 'were,' that of 'dwelling' or 'abiding.'

MAGIC THROUGH TANGIBLE THINGS

THE dread of being harmed through so intangible a thing as his name, which haunts the savage, is the extreme and more subtle form of the same dread which, for a like reason, makes him adopt precautions against cuttings of his hair, parings of his nails, his saliva, excreta, and the water in which his clothes--when he wears any--are washed, falling under the control of the sorcerer. Miss Mary Kingsley says that 'the fear of nail and hair clippings getting into the hands of evilly disposed persons is ever present to the West African: The Igalwa and other tribes will allow no one but a trusted friend to do their hair, and bits of nails or hair are carefully burnt or thrown away into a river. Blond., even that from a small cut on the finger. or from a fit of nose-bleeding, is most carefully covered up and stamped out if it has fallen on the earth. Blood is the life, and life in Africa means a spirit, hence the liberated blood is the liberated spirit, and liberated spirits are always whipping into people who don't want them. Crammed with Pagan superstitions, the Italian who is reluctant to trust a lock of his hair to another stands on the same plane as the barbarian. Sometimes, as was the custom among the Incas, and as is still the custom among Turks and Esthonians, the refuse of hair and nails is preserved so that the owner may have them at the resurrection of the body. In connection with this, one of my sons tells me that his Jamaican negro housekeeper speaks of the old-time blacks keeping their hair-cuttings to be put in a pillow in their coffins, and preserving the parings of their nails, because they would need them in the next world. It is a common superstition among ourselves that when children's teeth come out they should not be thrown away, lest the child has to seek for the lost tooth after death. On the other hand, it is an equally common practice to throw the teeth in the fire 'out of harm's way.'

But the larger number of practices give expression to the belief in what is known as 'sympathetic magic'; as we say, 'like cures like,' Or more appositely, in barbaric theory, 'kills like.' Things outwardly resembling one another are believed to possess the same qualities, effects being thereby brought about in the man himself by the production of like effects in things belonging to him, or in images or effigies of him. The Zulu sorcerers, when they have secured a portion of their victim's dress, will bury it in some secret place, so that, as it rots away, his life may decay. In the New Hebrides it was the common practice to hide nail-parings and cuttings of hair, and to give the remains of food carefully to the pigs. 'When the *mae* snake carried away a fragment of food into the place sacred to a spirit, the man who had eaten of the food would sicken as the fragment decayed. Brand tells that in a witchcraft trial in the seventeenth century, the accused confessed 'having buried a glove of the said Lord Henry in the ground, so that as the glove did rot and waste, the liver of the said lord might rot and waste'; and the New Britain sorcerer of to-day will burn a castaway banana skin, so that the man who carelessly left it unburied may die a tormenting death. A fever-stricken Australian native girl told the doctor who attended her that 'some moons back, when the Goulburn blacks were encamped near Melbourne, a young man named Gibberook came behind her and cut off a lock of her hair, and that she was sure he had buried it, and that it was rotting somewhere. Her marm-bu-la (kidney fat) was wasting away, and when the stolen hair had completely rotted she would die.' She added that her name had been lately cut on a tree by some wild black, and that was another sign of death. Her name was Murran, which means 'a leaf,' and the doctor afterwards found that the figure of leaves had been carved on a gum-tree as described by the girl. The sorceress said that the spirit of a black fellow had cut the figure on the tree.

The putting of sharp stones in the foot-tracks of an enemy is believed to maim him, as a nail is driven into a horse's footprint to lame him, while the chewing of a piece of wood is thought to soften the heart of a man with whom a bargain is being driven. Folk-medicine, the wide world through, is full of prescriptions based on sympathetic or antipathetic magic. Its doctrine of 'seals' or 'signatures' is expressed in the use of yellow flowers for jaundice, and of eye-bright for ophthalmia, while among the wonder-working roots there is the familiar mandrake of human shape, credited, in virtue of that resemblance, with magic power. In Umbria, where the peasants seek to nourish the consumptive on rosebuds and dew, the mothers take their children, wasted by sickness, to some boundary stone, perchance once sacred to Hermes, and pray to God to stay the illness or end the sufferer's life. The Cheroki make a decoction of the cone-flower for weak eyes because of the fancied resemblance of that plant to the strong-sighted eye of the deer; and they also drink an infusion of the tenacious burrs of the common beggars' lice, an Americai species of the genus *Desmodium*, to strengthen the memory. To ensure a fine voice, they boil crickets, and drink the liquor. In Suffolk and other parts of these islands, a common remedy for warts is to secretly pierce a snail or 'dodman with a gooseberry-bush thorn, rub the snail on the wart, and then bury it, so that, as it decays the wart may wither away.

Chinese doctors administer the head, middle or roots of plants, as the case may be, to cure the complaints of their patients in the head body, or legs. And with the practice of the Zulu medicine-man, who takes the bones of the oldest bull or dog of the tribe, giving scrapings of these to the sick, so that their lives may b prolonged to old age, we may compare that of doctors in the seventeenth century, who with lest logic, but perchance unconscious humour, gave their patients pulverised mummy to prolong their years. 'Mummie,' says Sir Thomas Browne, 'is become merchandise. Mizraim cures wounds, and Pharaoh is sold for balsams.'

In Plutarch's *Roman Questions*, which Dr. Jevons, in his valuable preface to the reprint of Philemon Holland's translation, remarks 'may fairly be said to be the earliest formal treatise written on the subject of folk-lore,' reference is made to the Roman customs of not completely clearing the table of food, and 'never putting foorth the light of a lampe, but suffering it to goe out of the owne accord.' These obviously come under the head of sympathetic magic, 'being safeguards against starvation and darkness.' In Melanesia, if a man wounds another with an arrow, he will drink hot juices and chew irritating leaves to bring about agony to the wounded, and he will keep his bow taut, pulling it at intervals to cause nerve-tension and tetanus in his victim. Here, though wide seas between them roll, we may compare the same philosophy of things at work. The 'sympathetic powder' used by Sir Kenelm Digby in the seventeenth century was believed to cure a wound if applied to the sword that inflicted it; and, to-day, the Suffolk farmer keeps the sickle with which he has cut himself free from rust, so that the wound may not fester. Here, too, lies the answer to the question that puzzled Plutarch. 'What is the reason that of all those things which be dedicate and consecrated to the gods, the custome is a Rome, that onely the spoiles of enemies conquered in the warres are neglected and suffered to run to decay in processe of time: neither is ther any reverence done unto them, nor repaired be they at any time when they wax olde?' Of course the custom is the outcome of the belief that the enemy's power waned as his armour rusted away.

Equally puzzling to Plutarch was the custom among Roman women 'of the most noble an auncient houses' to 'carry little moones upon their shoes.' These were of the nature of amulets, designed to deceive the lunacy-bringing moon spirit, so that it might enter the crescent charm instead of the wearer. 'The Chaldeans diverted the spirit of disease from the sick man by providing an image in the likeness of the spirit to attract the plague.' 'Make of it an image in his likeness (*i.e.* of Namtar, the plague); apply it to the living flesh of his body (i.e. of the sick man), may the malevolent Namtar who possesses him pass into the image.' But the reverse effect was more frequently the aim. A Chaldean tablet records the complaint of some victim, that 'he who enchants images has charmed away my life by image'; and Ibn Khaldun, an Arabian writer of the fourteenth century, describes how the Nabathean sorcerers of the Lower Euphrates made an image of the person whom they plotted to destroy. They transcribed his name on his effigy, uttered magic curses over it, and then, after divers other ceremonies, left the evil spirits to complete the fell work. In ancient Egyptian belief the ka of a living person could be transferred to a wax image by the repetition of formulae and there is no break in the long centuries between Accadian magic, which so profoundly influenced the West, and the practice of injuring a man through his image, which flourishes to-day. The Ojibways believe that 'by drawing the figure of any person in sand or clay, or by considering any object as the figure of a person, and then pricking it with a sharp stick or other weapon, or doing anything that would be done to the living body to cause pain or death, the person thus represented will suffer likewise.' King James I., in his *Daemonology*, Book is. ch. v., speaks of 'the devil teaching how to make pictures of wax or clay, that by roasting thereof the persons that they bear the name of may be continually melted or dried away by sickness; and, as showing the continuity of the idea, there are exhibited in the Pitt Rivers Museum at Oxford, besides similar objects from the Straits Settlements, a 'Corp Creidh' or 'clay body' from the Highlands, and a pig's heart from Devonshire, with pins stuck in them.

The assumed correspondence between physical phenomena and human actions is further shown in Dr Johnson's observation, when describing his visit to the Hebrides, that the peasants expect better crops by sowing their seed at the new moon; and he recalls from memory a precept annually given in the almanack, 'to kill hogs when the moon is waxing, that the bacon may prove the better in boiling.' With the ancient Roman custom of throwing images of the corn-spirit (doubtless substitutes of actual human offerings) into the river, so that the crops might be drenched with rain, we may compare the practice of the modern Servians and Thessalians, who strip a little girl naked, but wrap her completely in leaves and flowers, and then dance and sing round her, while bowls of water are poured over her to make the rain come. The life of man pulsates with the great heart of nature in many a touching superstition, as in the belief in the dependence of the earth's fertility on the vigour of the tree-spirit incarnated in the priest-king in the group which connects the waning of the days with the decline of human years; and, pathetically enough, in the widespread notion, of which Dickens makes use in *David Copperfield*, that life goes out with the ebb-tide.

'I was on the point of asking him if he knew me, when he tried to stretch out his arm, and said te me, distinctly, with a pleasant smile, "Barkis is willin'."'

'And, it being low water, he went out with the tide.'

The general idea has only to be decked ii another garb to fit the frame of mind which still reserves some pet sphere of nature for the operation of the special and the arbitrary. 'The narrower the range of man's knowledge of physical causes, the wider is the field which he hat to fill up with hypothetical causes of a metaphysical or supernatural character.'

We must not pass from these examples of belief in sympathetic connection, drawn from home at well as foreign sources, without reference to its significance in connection with food outside the prohibitions which are usually explained by the totem, that is, abstinence from the plant or animal which is regarded as the tribal ancestor.

Captain Wells, who was killed near Chicago in 1812, and who was celebrated for his valour among the Indians, was cut up into many parts, which were distributed among the allied tribes, so that all might have the opportunity of getting a taste of the courageous soldier. For it is a common belief among barbaric folk that by eating the flesh of a brave man a portion of his courage is absorbed. The Botecudos sucked the blood of living victims that they might imbibe spiritual force, and among the Brazilian natives the first food given to a child, when weaning it, was the flesh of an enemy. Cannibalism, the origin of which is probably due to a scarcity of animal food, therefore acquires this superadded motive, in which also lies the explanation of the eating of, or abstaining from, the flesh of certain animals. The lion's flesh gives courage, the deer's flesh causes timidity; and in more subtle form of the same idea, barbaric hunters will abstain from oil lest the game slip through their fingers. Contrariwise, the Hessian lad thinks that he may escape the conscription by carrying a baby girl's cap in his pocket: a symbolic way of repudiating manhood.

Most suggestive of all is the extension of the idea to the eating of the slain god, whereby his spirit is imbibed, and communion with the unseen secured. To quote Mr. Frazer, the savage believes that 'by eating the body of the god he shares in the god's attributes and powers; and when the god is a corn-god, the corn is his proper body; when he is a vine-god, the juice of the grape is his blood; and so, by eating the bread and drinking the wine, the worshipper partakes of the real body and blood of his god. Thus the drinking of wine in the rite of a vine-god, like Dionysus, is not an act of revelry; it is a solemn sacrament.' Experience shows that people possessing intelligence above the ordinary often fail to see the bearing of one set of facts upon another set, especially if the application can be' made to their traditional beliefs, whether these are only mechanically held, or ardently defended. It is, therefore, not wholly needless to point out that Mr. Frazer's explanation is to be extended to the rites attaching to Christianity, transubstantiation being, laterally or lineally, the descendant of the barbaric idea of eating the god, whereby the communicant becomes a 'partaker of the divine nature.' In connection with this we may cite Professor Robertson Smith's remark, that a notable application of the idea of eating the flesh or drinking the blood of another being, so that a man absorbs its nature or life into his own, is the rite of blood-brotherhood, the simplest form of which is in two men opening their veins and sucking one another's blood. 'Thenceforth their lives are not two, but one. ' Among the Unyamuezi the ceremony is performed by cutting incisions in each other's legs and letting the blood trickle together. Fuller reference. to this widely diffused rite will, however, have more fitting place later on, when treating of the custom of the exchange of names which, as will be seen, often goes with it. Belief in virtue inhering in the dead man's body involves belief in virtue in his belongings, in which is the key to the belief in the efficacy of relics as vehicles of supernatural power. Here the continuity is clearly traceable. There is no fundamental difference between the savage who carries about with him the skull-bones of his ancestor as a charm or seat of oracle, and the Buddhist who places the relics of holy men beneath the tope, or the Catholic who deposits the fragments of saints or martyrs within the altar which their presence sanctifies; while the mother, treasuring her dead child's lock of hair, witnesses to the vitality of feelings drawn from perennial springs in human nature. Well-nigh every relic which the Church safeguards beneath her shrines, or exhibits, at stated seasons, for the adoration of the crowd, is spurious, yet no amount of ridicule thrown on these has impaired the credulity whose strength lies in the dominance of the wish to believe over the desire to know.

In 'Whuppity Stoorie' the widow and the witch 'watted thooms' over their bargain. Man's saliva plays a smaller, but by no means inactive, part in his superstitions. A goodly-sized book might be written on the history and ethnic distribution of the customs connected with it. Employed as vehicle of blessing or cursing, of injury or cure, by peoples intellectually as far apart as the Jews, the South Sea Islanders, the medieval Christians, and the Central Africans of to-day, the potencies of this normally harmless secretion have been most widely credited. Among ourselves it is a vehicle of one of the coarsest forms of assault, or the degenerate representative of the old luck-charm in the spitting on money by the cabman or the costermonger. Among certain barbaric races, however, the act expresses the kindliest feeling and the highest compliment. Consul Petherick says that a Sudanese chief, after grasping his hand, spat on it, and then did the like to his face, a form of salute which the consul returned with interest, to the delight of the recipient. Among the Masai the same custom is universal; and while it is bad form to kiss a lady, it is *comme il faut* to spit on her authority who reports this adds an account of certain generative virtues with which saliva, especially if administered by a white man, is accredited. But it is as a prophylactic, notably in the form of fasting spittle, and as a protection against sorcery and all forms of black magic, that we meet with frequent references to it in ancient writers, and in modern books of travel 'Spittle,' says Brand, 'was esteemed a charm against all kinds of fascination, notably against the evil eye, the remedy for which, still in vogue among the Italians, is to spit three times upon the breast, as did the urban maiden in Theocritus when she refused her rustic wooer. It came out in the course of a murder trial at Philippopolis, that the Bulgarians believe that spitting gives immunity from the consequences of perjury. An example of its use in benediction occurs, as when the Abomel of Alzpirn spat on his clergy and laity; but more familiar are the cases of its application in baptism and name-giving. Seward says that 'the custom of nurses lustrating the children by spittle was one of the ceremonies used on the Dies Nominalis, the day the child was named; so that there can be no doubt of the Papists deriving this custom from the heathen nurses and grandmothers. They have indeed christened it, as it were, by flinging in some Scriptural expressions; but then they have carried it to a more filthy extravagance by daubing it on the nostrils of adults as well as of children.' Ockley tells that when Hasan was born, his grandfather, Mohammed, spat in his mouth as he named him; and Mungo Park thus describes the name-giving ceremony among the Mandingo people. 'A child is named when it is seven or eight days old. The ceremony commences by shaving the head. The priest offers a prayer, in which he solicits the blessing of God upon the child and all the company, and then whispering a few sentences in the child's ear, spits three times in his face, after which, pronouncing his name aloud, be returns the child to its mother.'

All which, of course, has vital connection with the belief in inherent virtue in saliva, and therefore with the widespread group of customs which have for their object the prevention of its falling within the power of the sorcerer. Suabian folk-medicine prescribes that the saliva should at once be trodden into the ground lest some evil-disposed. person use it for sorcery. As the result of extensive acquaintance with the North American Indians, Captain Bourke says that all of them are careful to spit into their cloaks or blankets and Kane adds his testimony that the natives of Columbia River are never seen to spit without carefully stamping out the saliva. This they do lest an enemy should find it, and work injury through it. The chief officer of the 'king' of Congo receives the royal saliva in a rag, which he doubles up and kisses; while in Hawaii the guardianship of the monarch's expectorations was intrusted only to a chief of high rank, who held the dignified office of spittoon-bearer to the king, and who, like his fellow-holders of the same trust under other Polynesian rulers, buried the saliva beyond the reach of malicious medicine-men. Finally, as bearing on the absence of any delimiting lines between a man's belongings, there may be cited Brand's reference to Debrio. He 'portrays the manners and ideas of the continent, and mentions that upon those hairs which come out of the head in combing they spit thrice before they throw them away.'

The reluctance of savages to have their portraits taken is explicable when brought into relation with the group of confused ideas under review. Naturally, the man thinks that virtue has gone out of him, that some part of his vulnerable self is put at the mercy of his fellows, when he sees his 'counterfeit presentment' on a sheet of paper, or peering from out magic glass. The reluctance of unlettered people among ourselves to have their likenesses taken is not uncommon. From Scotland to Somerset there comes evidence about the ill-health or ill-luck which followed the camera, of folks who 'took bad and died' after being 'a-tookt.' These facts will remove any surprise at Catlin's well known story of the accusation brought against him by the Yukons that he had made buffaloes scarce by putting so many pictures of them in his book.

THE examples of belief in a man's tangible belongings as vehicles of black magic will have paved the way for examples of like belief about intangible things, as shadows, reflections, and names.

The savage knows nothing of the action of the laws of interference of light or sound. The echoes of voices which the hillside flings back; the reflections which water casts; and the shadows which follow or precede, and which lengthen or shorten, a man's figure; all unite in supporting the theory of another self. The Basuto avoids the river-bank, lest, as his shadow falls on the water, a crocodile may seize it, and harm the owner. In Wetar Island. near Celebes.. the magicians profess to make a man ill by spearing or stabbing his shadow; the Arabs believe that if a hyena treads on a shadow, it deprives the man of the power of speech; and in modern Roumania the ancient custom of burying a victim as sacrifice to the earth-spirit under any new structure, has survival in the builder enticing some passer-by to draw near, so that his shadow is thrown on the foundation-stone, the belief being that he will die within the year. New England tribes call the soul *chermung* or shadow, and civilised speech indicates community of idea in the *skia* of the Greeks, the *manes* or *umbra* of the Romans, and the *shade* of our own language. But any due enlargement of this department of the subject would fill no small volume, since it involves the story of the origin and development of spiritual ideas ruling the life of man from the dawn of thought; and, moreover, those ideas find sufficing illustration in savage notions about names.

Starting at the bottom of the scale, we have Mr. Brough Smyth's testimony that the Victoria black-fellows are very unwilling to tell their real names, and that this reluctance is due to the fear of putting themselves at the mercy of sorcerers. Backhouse says that the Tasmanians showed great dislike to their names being mentioned.

Among the Tshi-speaking tribes of West Africa, 'a man's name is always concealed from all but his nearest relatives, and to other persons he is always known by an assumed name,' a nickname, as we should say. The Ewe-speaking peoples 'believe in a real and material connection between a man and his name, and that, by means of the name, injury may be done to' the man.' Mr. Im Thurn says that, although the Indians of British Guiana have an intricate system of names, it is 'of little use in that the owners have a very strong objection to telling or using them, apparently on the ground that the name is part of the man, and that he who knows it has part of the owner of that name in his power. To avoid any danger of spreading knowledge of their names, one Indian, therefore, usually addresses another only according to the relationship of the caller and the called. But an Indian is just as unwilling to tell his proper name to a white man as to an Indian; and as, of course, between those two there is no relationship the term for which can serve as a proper name, the Indian asks the European to give him a name, which is usually written on a piece of paper by the donor, and shown by the Indian to any white who asks his name.' The Indians of British Columbia--and the prejudice 'appears to pervade all tribes alike'--dislike telling their names; thus you never get a man's right name from himself, but they will tell each other's names without hesitation. In correspondence with this, the Abipones of South America would nudge their neighbour to answer for them when any one among them was asked his name; and the natives of the Fiji Islands would get any third party who might be present to answer as to their names. An Indian asked Dr. Kane whether his wish to know his name arose from a desire to steal it; and the Araucanians would not allow their names to be told to strangers lest these should be used in sorcery. Among the Ojibways, husbands and wives never told each other's names, and children were warned that they would stop growing if they repeated their own names. Of the Abipones just named, Dobriz-hoffer reports that they would knock at his door at night, and, when asked who was there, would not answer for fear of letting their names be known to any evilly-disposed listener. A like motive probably explains the reluctance of which Gregor speaks in his *Folk-Lore of the North-East of Scotland*, when 'folk calling at a house of the better class on business with the master or mistress had a very strong dislike to tell their names to the servant who admitted them.' While these sheets are passing through the press, my friend Mr. W. B. Yeats hands me a letter from an Irish correspondent, who tells of a fairy-haunted old woman living in King's County. Her tormentors, whom she calls the 'Fairy Band of Shinrone,' come from Tipperary. They pelt her with invisible missiles, hurl abuse at her, and rail against her family, both the dead and the living, until she is driven well-nigh mad. And all this spite is manifested because they cannot find out her name, for if they could learn that, she would be in their power. Sometimes sarcasm or chaff is employed, and a nickname is given her to entrap her into telling her real name,--all which she freely talks about, often with fits of laughter. But the fairies trouble her most at night, coming in through the wall over her bed-head, which is no laughing matter; and then, being a good Protestant, she recites chapters and verses from the Bible to charm them away. And although she has been thus plagued for years, she still holds her own against the 'band of Shinrone.' Speaking in general terms on this name-concealment custom, Captain Bourke says that 'the name of an American Indian is a sacred thing, never to be divulged by the owner himself without due consideration. One may ask a warrior of any tribe to give his name, and the question will be met with either a point-blank refusal, or the more diplomatic evasion that he cannot understand what is wanted of him. The moment a friend approaches, the warrior first will whisper what is wanted, and the friend can tell the name, receiving a reciprocation of the courtesy from the inquirer.' Grinnell says that 'many Blackfeet. change their names every season. Whenever a Blackfoot counts a new coup (i.e. some deed of bravery), he is entitled to a new name,' in the same way that among ourselves a successful general or admiral sinks his name when raised to the peerage. 'A Blackfoot will never tell his name if he can avoid it, in the belief that if he should reveal it, he would be unlucky in all his undertakings.' The warriors of the Plains Tribes 'used to assume agnomens or battle-names, and I have known some of them who had enjoyed as many as four or five; but the Apache name, once conferred, seems to remain through life, except in the case of the medicine-men, who, I have always suspected, change their names on assuming their profession, much as a professor of learning in China is said to do,' and, it may be added, as among high dignitaries of the church, members of ecclesiastical orders, and so forth. But of this more presently. The foregoing reference to names of warriors permits the inclusion of a story told by Fraser in his *Tour to the Himalayas*. In one of the despatches intercepted during our war with Nepaul, Gooree Sah had sent orders to 'find out the name of the commander of the British army; write it upon a piece of paper: take it and some rice and turmeric; say the great incantation three times; having said it, send for some plum-tree wood, and therewith burn it.' There is a story in the annals of British conquest in India to the effect that General Lake took a city with surprisingly little resistance, because his name signified in the native language 'Crocodile,' and there was an oracle that the city would be captured by that reptile. Phonetic confusion explains the honours paid to Commissioner Gubbins by the natives of Oude; Govinda being the favourite name of Krishna, the popular incarnation of Vishnu.

Mr. J. H. Collens, in his *Guide to Trinidad*, published in 1887, tells the following story--

A doctor in a remote district had one day assembled a number of negro children for vaccination. In the course of his duties he came to a little girl, when the following conversation ensued with the mother:--

Doctor. Are you the child's mother?

WOMAN. Yes, sir--is me darter.

D And what is your name?

W. Is me name?

D. (rather impatiently). Yes; I asked you what is your name?

W (hesitatingly). Dey does caal me Sal.

D. Well; Sal what?

W (assuringly, but with a suspicious side-glance at a neighbour who is intently taking all in). Dey does allus caal me Sal.

D. (getting desperate). Oh, botheration! will you tell me your proper name or not?

W. (with much reluctance approaching the doctor, whispers in the lowest possible tone of voice). Deiphine Segard.

D. (with intense disgust). Then why couldn't you say so?

Mr. Collens remarks that his 'medical friend

now bears these little passages with more equanimity, for he has gained experience, and knows that the reason why the woman was so reluctant to utter her name aloud was that she believed she had an enemy in the room who would take advantage of the circumstance if she got hold of her true name, and would work her all manner of harm. It is a fact that these people (the negro population of Trinidad) sometimes actually forget the names of their near relations from hearing and using them so little.'

With this group of examples chosen from widely sundered sources, and with the ever-growing evidence of continuity of old ideas lurking in the veriest trifles, it may not be so far-fetched as at first sight it seems, to detect traces of the avoidance-superstition in the game-rhyme familiar to our childhood -

'What is your name?
Pudding and tame.
If you ask me again I'll tell you the same.'

Ellis says, 'It appears strange that the birth-name only, and not an alias, should be believed capable of carrying some of the personality of the bearer elsewhere, since the latter preserves the subjective connection just as well as the real name. But the native view seems to be that the alias does not really belong to the man.' This view, which is universal through every stage of culture, takes practical effect from the time that the child is born and made the subject of name-giving ceremonies. In civilised communities, the 'baptismal name is the real name, the name registered in heaven,' and this belief is an integral part of the general body of customs which have for their object the protection of the infant from maleficent agents at the critical period of birth. 'The ancients,' says Aubrey, 'had a solemne time of giving names,--the equivalent to our christening.' Barbaric, Pagan, and Christian folk-lore is full of examples of the importance of naming and other birth-ceremonies, in the belief that the child's life is at the mercy of evil spirits watching the chance of casting spells upon it, of demons covetous to possess it, and of fairies eager to steal it, and leave a 'changeling' in its place. This last-named superstition as to theft of the newly born by the 'little folk' is availed of as subject of humorous incident by the writer of the old mystery play of the 'Shepherds' (*Secunda Pastorum*), in the Towneley Collection. While all the hinds except Mak have fallen asleep, he steals home with a sheep, which he pops into the cradle, telling his wife to feign lying-in. Then he returns to his mates, and, shamming sleep, says that they have roused him from a dream that his wife has given birth to a 'yong lad,' and so makes excuse to hasten to her.

When he is gone, the sheep is missed, whereupon the shepherds follow Mak home, and are bidden to 'speke soft' because of the 'seke woman.' They are thus put off guard, but on leaving, one of them remembers that no gift had been made to the child, so they return for that kindly office. Despite Mak's entreaties not to, disturb the sleep of the 'lyttle day starne,' they 'lyft up the clowtt,' and discover strange likeness between the babe and the 'shepe.' Both Mak and his wife declare this metamorphosis to be the maliceful work of fairies, the woman saying that the boy

'Was takyn with an elfe.
I saw it myself
When the clok stroke tweilf
Was he forshapyn' (transformed).

'The hour of midnight,' says Brand, 'was looked on by our forefathers as the season when this species of sorcery was generally performed.'

In Ireland the belief in changelings is as strong as it was in pre-Christian times; both there and in Scotland the child is carefully watched till the rite of baptism is performed, fishermen's nets being sometimes spread over the curtain openings to prevent the infant being carried off; while in West Sussex it is considered unlucky to divulge a child's intended name before baptism. This reminds us of the incident in the Moray story, Nicht Nought Nothing, in which the queen would not christen the bairn till the king came back, saying, 'We will just call him Nicht Nought Nothing until his father comes home.'

Brand says that among Danish women precaution against evil spirits took the form of putting garlick, bread, salt, or some steel instrument as amulets about the house before laying the newborn babe in the cradle. Henderson says that in Scotland 'the little one's safeguard is held to lie in the placing of some article of clothing belonging to the father near the cradle,' while in South China a pair of the father's trousers are put near the bedstead, and a word-charm pinned to them, so that all evil influences may pass into them instead of harming the babe, and in New Britain a charm is always hung in the house to secure the child from like peril. In Ruthenia it is believed that if a wizard knows a man's baptismal name he can transform him by a mere effort of will. Parkyns says that it is the custom in Abyssinia 'to conceal the real name by which a person is baptized, and to call him only by a sort of nickname which his mother gives him on leaving the church. The baptismal names in Abyssinia are those of saints, such as Son of St. George, Slave of the Virgin, Daughter of Moses, etc. Those given by the mother are generally expressive of maternal vanity regarding the appearance or anticipated merits of the child. The reason for the concealment of the Christian name is that the Bouda cannot harm a person whose real name he does not know.' Should he, however, have learned the true name of his victim, he adopts a method of which illustrations have been given in the references to sympathetic magic. 'He takes a particular kind of straw, and muttering something over it bends it into a circle, and places it under a stone The person thus doomed is taken ill at the very moment of the bending of the straw, and should it by accident snap under the operation, the result of the attack will be the death of the patient.' Parkyns adds that in Abyssinia all blacksmiths are looked upon as wizards or Boudas. Among the many characters in which the devil appears is that of Wayland the Smith, the northern Vulcan, but perhaps the repute attaching to the Boudas has no connection with that conception, and may be an example of the barbaric belief in the magic power of iron to which allusion has been made. They are credited with the faculty of being able to turn themselves into hyenas and other wild beasts, so that few people will venture to molest or offend a black smith. 'In all church services in Abyssinia, particularly in prayers for the dead, the baptismal name must be used. How they manage to hid it I did not learn; possibly by confiding it only to the priest.' Mr. Theodore Bent says that it is a custom in the Cyclades to call a child Iron or Dragon or some other such name before christening takes place, the object being to frighten away the evil spirits. Travelling east wards, we find the Hindu belief that when i child is born an invisible spirit is born with it and unless the mother keeps one breast tied up for forty days, while she feeds the child with the other (in which case the spirit dies of hunger the child grows up with the endowment of the evil eye. Two names are given at birth, one secret and used only for ceremonial purposes, and the other for ordinary use. The witch, if she learns the real name, can work her evil charms through it. Hence arises the use of many contractions and perversions of the real name, and many of the nicknames which are generally given to children. Among the Algonquin tribes children are usually named by the old woman of the family, often with reference to some dream; but this real name is kept mysteriously secret, and what commonly passes for it is a mere nickname, such as 'Little Fox' or 'Red Head.' School-craft says that the true name of the famous Pocahontas, 'La Belle Sauvage,' whose pleadings saved the life of the heroic Virginian leader, John Smith, was Matokes. 'This was concealed from the English in a superstitious fear of hurt by them if her name was known.'

It is well known that in Roman Catholic countries the name-day wholly supersedes the birthday in importance; and, as the foregoing examples testify, the significance attached to the name brings into play a number of causes operating in the selection, causes grouped round belief in omens, and in meanings to be attached to certain events, of which astrology is a world-wide interpreter.

Among the Red Indians 'the giving of name' to children is a solemn matter, and one in which the medicine-man should always be consulted The Plains Tribes named their children at the moment of piercing their ears, which should occur at the first sun-dance after their birth, or rather, as near their first year as possible.' At the birth of every Singhalese baby its horoscope is cast by an astrologer; and so highly is this document esteemed, that even in the hour of death more reliance is placed upon it than on the symptoms of the patient! Again, the astrologer is called in to preside at the baby's 'rice-feast, when some grains of rice are first placed in it mouth. He selects for the little one a name which is compounded from the name of the ruling planet of that moment. This name he tells only to the father, who whispers it low in the baby's ear; no one else must know it, and, like the Chinese 'infantile name,' this 'rice-name' is never used lest sorcerers should hear it and be able to work malignant spells.

In every department of human thought evidence of the non-persistence of primitive ideas is the exception rather than the rule. Scratch the epiderm of the civilised man, and the barbarian is found in the derm. In proof of which, there are more people who believe in Zadkiel's *Vox Stellarum* than in the *Nautical Almanac*; and rare are the households where the *Book of Dreams and Fortune-Teller* are not to be found in the kitchen. The Singhalese caster of nativities has many representatives in the West, and there may lie profit in the reminder of the shallow depth to which knowledge of the orderly sequence of things has yet penetrated in the many. Societies and serials for the promulgation of astrology exist and flourish among us; Zadkiel boasts his circulation of a hundred thousand, and vaunts the fulfilment of his Delphh prophecies; while the late Astronomer-Royal, Sir George Airy, was pestered, as his successor probably is, with requests to work the planets accompanied by silver wherewith to cross his expert palm. There lies before me a book entitled Kabalistic Astrology, in which, darkened by pages of pseudo-philosophic jargon, a theory is formulated on 'the power of Names and Numbers,' 'all names being essentially numbers, and vice versa. 'A name is a mantram, an invocation, a spell, a charm. It gains its efficacy from the fact that, in pronunciation, certain vibrations, corresponding to the mass-chord of the name, are set up; not only in the atmosphere, but also in the more ethereal substance, referred to by a modern philosopher as "mind-stuff," whose modifications form the basis of changes of thought. This is evident to us in the fact that names import to our minds certain characteristics, more or less definite according to the acuteness of our psychometric sense How different, for example, are the impressions conveyed to us the names "Percy," Horatio," "Ralph,"" Eva," and "Ruth." Seeing then this difference, it will not seem wholly improbable that a difference of fortune and destiny should go along with them.' The evidence of astrological logic which this last sentence affords is on a par with what follows throughout the fatuous volume. All names are numbers, and each letter in the name has its numerical and astral value by which can be known what planets were in the ascendant at the time of birth of the person whose horoscope is being cast. Such is the stuff that still 'leads captive silly' folk. The old astrology had a certain quality of nobleness about it. As Comte has justly said, it was an attempt to frame a philosophy of history by reducing the seemingly capricious character of human actions within the domain of law. It strove to establish a connection between these actions and the motions of the heavenly bodies which were deified by the ancients and credited with personal will directing the destiny of man. But the new astrology is the vulgarest travesty of the old.

While among the Mordvins of the Caucasus and other peoples accident or whim determines the child's name, among the Tshi-speaking tribes of West Africa this is given at the moment of birth and derived from the day of the week when that event happens. After being washed, charms are bound round the child to avert evil. Throughout Australia the custom of deriving the name from some slight circumstance prevails. 'Like the nomadic Arabs and the Kaffirs, a sign is looked for, and the appearance of a kangaroo or an emu at the time of birth, or the occurrence of that event near some particular spot, or under the shelter of a tree, decides the infant's name. This name is not the one by which a man will be known in after life. Another is given him on his initiation to rank in the tribe; and, if his career should be marked by any striking event, he will then receive a fitting designation, and his old name will be perhaps forgotten. Or, if he has had conferred on him, on arriving at manhood, a name similar to that of any one who, dies, it is changed by his tribe.' With this may be compared the Aino abstention from giving the name of either parent to the child, because, when they are dead, they are not to be 'mentioned without tears,' and also the feeling in the North of England against perpetuating a favourite baptismal name when death has snatched away its first bearer. 'The clan of the Manlii at Rome avoided giving the name of Marcus to any son born in the clan. We may infer from this that the possession of the name was once thought to be bound up with evil consequences,' and this notwithstanding the legend that the name-avoidance was due to Marius Manlius--who proved himself the saviour of the city when the clamouring of geese aroused the garrison of the Capitol to a scaling attack by the Gauls--being afterwards put to death for plotting to found a monarchy.

The custom of name-giving from some event has frequent reference in the Old Testament, as, for example, in Genesis xxx. 11, where Leah's maid gives birth to a son; 'And she said, A troop cometh, and she called his name, Gad.' So Rachel, dying in childbed, calls the babe Ben-oni, 'son of sorrow,' but the father changes his name to Ben-jamin, 'son of the right hand.' The Nez Percés obtain their names in several ways, one of the more curious being the sending of a child in his tenth or twelfth year to the mountains, where he fasts and watches for something to appear to him in a dream and give him a name. On the success or failure of the vision which the empty stomach is designed to secure, his fortunes are believed to depend. No one questions him on his return, the matter being regarded as sacred, and only years hence, when he may have done something to be proud of, will he reveal his name to trusted friends. Of course, throughout his life he is known to his fellow-tribesmen by some nickname. The Maoris had an interesting baptismal or lustration ceremony, during which the priest repeated a long list of ancestral names. When the child sneezed, the name which was then being uttered was chosen, and the priest, as he pronounced it, sprinkled the child with a small branch 'of the karamu which was stuck upright in the water.'

In East Central Africa the birth-name is changed when the initiatory rites are performed, after which it must never be mentioned. Mr. Duff-Macdonald says that it is a terrible way of teasing a Wayao to point to a little boy and ask if he remembers what was his name when he was about the size of that boy. Miss Mary Kingsley confirms these reports of the silence and secrecy on the part of the initiated; and in an unpublished manuscript on the customs in Loango, which came into my hands, Mr. Dennett makes the interesting and significant statement that on the initiation of a youth into the tribal mysteries when he reaches manhood, he lies down in his forest retreat as if dead, and on rising takes a new name. Here we seem scarcely a step removed from the ritual of the Roman Catholic Church, when the Miserere is chanted, and a pall flung over the nun who takes the veil and effaces her old self under another name.

In fact, these correspondences bring us face to face with the large question of the origin of the rites and ceremonies of civilised faiths which show no essential difference in character from those in practice among barbaric races; rites and ceremonies gathering round the chief events, as birth, maturity, marriage, and death. Those who contend, for example, that the ordinance of baptism in the Christian Church is of divine authority, thus possessing warrant which makes 'it wholly a thing apart from the lustrations and naming-customs which are so prominent a feature of barbaric life, will not be at pains to compare the one with the other. If they do, it will be rather to assume that the lower is a travesty of the higher, in the spirit of the Roman Catholic missionaries, who on seeing the tonsured Buddhist monks with all the apparatus of rosaries, bells, holy water, and relics, believed that the devil, as arch-deceiver, had tempted these ecclesiastics to dress themselves in the clothes of Christians, and mock their solemn rites. The majority of Christendom still attaches enormous importance to infant baptism, an importance which is shared, for less precise reasons, by rustics, who believe that 'children never thrive till they're christened,' and that the night air thrills to the cry of the homeless souls of the unbaptized. That superstitions of this order should be rampant among the unlettered, evidences their pagan origin rather than the infiltration of sacerdotal theories of baptismal regeneration and of the doom of the unchristened. But between the believers in these theories, and those who see in the ritual of the higher religions the persistence of barbaric ideas, there will be agreement when the poles meet the equator. The explanation which the evolutionist has to give falls into line with what is known and demonstrated about the arrest of human development by the innate conservatism aroused when doubt disturbs the settled order of things. Rites, like their dispensers, may change their name, but not their nature, and in the ceremonies of civil and religious society we find no inventions, only survivals more or less elaborated. The low intellectual environment of man's barbaric past was constant in his history for thousands of years, and his adaptation thereto was complete. The intrusion of the scientific method in its application to man's whole nature disturbed that equilibrium. But this, as yet, only within the narrow area of the highest culture. Like the lower life-forms that constitute the teeming majority of organisms, and that have undergone little, if any, change during millions of years, the vaster number of mankind have remained but slightly, if at all, modified. The keynote of evolution is adaptation, not continuous development, and this is illustrated, both physically and mentally, by man. Therefore, the superstitions that still dominate human life, even in so-called civilised centres and 'high places,' are no stumbling-blocks to the student of history. He accounts for their persistence, and the road of inquiry is cleared. Man being a unit, not a duality, thought and feeling are, in the last resort, in harmony, as are the elements that make up the universe which includes him. But the exercise of feeling has been active from the beginning of his history, while thought, speaking comparatively, has but recently had free play. So far as its influence on the modern world goes, and this with long periods of arrest between, we may say that it began, at least in the domain of scientific naturalism, with the Ionian philosophers, twenty-four centuries ago. And these are but as a day in the passage of prehistoric ages. In other words, man wondered long chiliads before he reasoned, because feeling travels along the line of least resistance, while thought, or the challenge by inquiry, with its assumption that there may be two sides to a question, must pursue a path obstructed by the dominance of taboo and custom, by the force of imitation, and by the strength of prejudice, passion, and fear. 'It is not error,' Turgot wrote, in a saying that every champion of a new idea should have ever in letters of flame before his eyes, 'which opposes the progress of truth; it is indolence, obstinacy, the spirit of routine, everything that favours inaction.'

In these causes lies the explanation of the persistence of the primitive; the causes of the general conservatism of human nature,

'Born into life, in vain,
Opinions, those or these,
Unalter'd to retain,
The obstinate mind decrees,'

as in the striking illustration cited in Heine's *Travel-Pictures*. 'A few years ago Bullock dug' up an ancient stone idol in Mexico, and the next day he found that it had been crowned during the night with flowers. And yet the Spaniard had exterminated the old Mexican religion with, fire and sword, and for three centuries had been engaged in ploughing and harrowing their minds and implanting the seed of Christianity '

The causes of error and delusion, and of the spiritual nightmares of olden time, being made clear, there is begotten a generous sympathy with that which empirical notions of human nature attributed to wilfulness or to man's fall from a high estate. For superstitions which are the outcome of ignorance can only awaken pity. Where the corrective of knowledge is absent, we see that it could not be otherwise. And thereby we learn that the art of life largely consists in that control of the emotions, and that diversion of them into wholesome channels, which the intellect, braced with the latest knowledge and with freedom in the application of it, can alone effect.

These remarks have direct bearing on the inferences to be drawn from the examples gathered from barbaric and civilised sources. For those examples fail in their intent if they do not indicate the working of the law of continuity in the spiritual as in the material sphere. Barbaric birth and baptism customs, and the importance attached to the name with accompanying invocation and other ceremonies, explain without need of import of other reasons, the existence of similar practices, impelled by similar ideas, in civilised society. The priest who christens the child 'in the Name of the Father, Son, and Holy Ghost' is the lineal descendant, the true apostolic successor, of the medicine-man. He may deny the spiritual father who begat him, and vaunt his descent from St. Peter. But the first Bishop of Rome, granting that title to the apostle, was himself a parvenu compared to the barbaric priest who uttered his incantations on the hill now crowned by the Vatican. The story of the beginnings of his order in a prehistoric past is a sealed book to the priest. For, in East and West alike, his studies have run between the narrow historical lines enclosing only such material as is interpreted to support the preposterous claims to the divine origin of his office which the multitude have neither the courage to challenge nor the knowledge to refute. Did those studies run on the broad lines laid down~ by anthropology, the sacerdotal upholders of those claims would be compelled to abandon their pretensions and thus sign the death-warrant of their caste. The modern sacerdotalist represents in the ceremony of baptism the barbaric belief in the virtue of water as--in some way equally difficult to both medicine-man and priest to define--a vehicle of supernatural efficacy. In the oldest fragment of Hebrew song the stream is addressed as a living being, and the high authority of the late Professor Robertson Smith may be cited for the statement that the Semitic peoples, to whom water, especially flowing water, was the deepest object of reverence and worship, regarded it not merely as the dwelling-place of spirits, but as itself a living organism. That has been the barbaric idea about it everywhere; and little wonder. For the primitive mind associates life with motion; and if in rolling stone and waving branch it sees not merely the home and haunt of spirit, but spirit itself, how much more so in tumbling cataract, swirling rapid, and tossing sea, swallowing or rejecting alike the victim and the offering. Birthplace of life itself, and ever life's necessity; mysterious fluid endowed with cleansing and healing qualities, the feeling that invests it can only be refined, it cannot perish. And we therefore think with sympathy of that 'divine honour' which Gildas tells us out forefathers 'paid to wells and streams'; of the food-bringing rivers which, in the old Celtic faith, were 'mothers'; of the eddy in which the water-demon lurked; of the lakes ruled by lonely queens; of the nymphs who were the presiding genii of wells. Happily, the Church treated this old phase of nature-worship tenderly, adapting what it could not abolish, substituting the name of Madonna or saint for the pagan presiding deity of the spring. Most reasonable therefore, is the contention that the barbaric lustrations re appear in the rite at Christian fonts; that the brush of the pagan temple sprinkles the faithful with holy water, as it still sprinkles with benediction the horses in the *Palio* or prize races at Siena; and that the leprous Naaman repairing to the Jordan, together with the sick waiting their turn on the margin of Bethesda, have their correspondences in the children dipped in wells to be cured of rickets, in the dragging of lunatics through deep water to restore their reason, and in the cripples who travel by railway to bathe their limbs in the well of St. Winifred in Flintshire. The influence which pagan symbolism had on Christian art and doctrine has interesting illustration in a mosaic of the sixth century at Ravenna, representing the baptism of Jesus. The water flows from an inverted urn, held by a venerable figure typifying the river-god of the Jordan, with reeds growing beside his head, and snakes coiling round it.

TABOO is the dread tyrant of savage life. Among civilised peoples, under the guise of customs whose force is stronger than law, it rules in larger degree than most persons care to admit. But among barbaric communities it puts a ring. fence round the simplest acts, regulates all intercourse by the minutest codes, and secures obedience to its manifold prohibitions by threats of punishment to be inflicted by magic and other apparatus of the invisible. It is the Inquisition of the lower culture, only more terrible and effective than the infamous 'Holy Office.' Nowhere, perhaps, does it exert more constant sway than in the series of customs which prohibit (a) persons related in certain degrees by blood or marriage from addressing one another by name, or from even looking at one another, and which further prohibit (b) the utterance of the names of individuals of high rank, as priests and kings, as also (c) of the dead, and (d) of gods and spiritual beings generally.

TABOO BETWEEN RELATIVES

Among the Central Australians a man may not marry or speak to his mother-in-law. He may speak to his mother at all times, but not to his sister if she be younger than himself. A father may not speak to his daughter after she becomes a woman. The name of his father-in-law is taboo to the Dyak of Borneo, and among the Omahas of North America the father- and mother-in-law do not speak to their son-in-law or mention his name. The names of mothers-in-law are never uttered by the Apache, and it would be very improper to ask for them by name. In the Bougainville Straits the men would only utter the names of their wives in a low tone, as though it was not the proper thing to speak of women by name to others. In East Africa, among the Barea, the wife never utters the name of her husband, or eats in his presence; and even among the Beni Amer, where the women have extensive privileges and great social power, the wife is still not allowed to eat in the husband's presence, and mentions his name only before strangers. In the Banks Islands the rules as to avoidance are very minute. 'A man who sits and talks with his wife's father will not mention his name, much less the name of his mother-in-law; and the like applies to the wife, who, further, will on no account name her daughter's husband.' But these prohibitions are not found in all the Melanesian islands. Among the Sioux or Dacotas the father- or mother-in-law must not call their sons-in-law by name, and *vice versa*; while the Indians east of the Rockies regard it as indecent for either fathers- or mothers-in-law to look at, or speak- to, their sons- or daughters-in-law. It was considered a gross breach of propriety among the Blackfoot tribe for a man to meet his mother-in-law; and if by any mischance he did so, or, what was worse, if he spoke to her, she demanded a heavy payment, which he was compelled to make. In New Britain a man must under no circumstances speak to his mother-in-law; he must go miles out of his way not to meet her, and the penalty for breaking an oath is to be forced to shake hands With her. In some parts of Australia the mother-in-law does not allow the son-in-law to see her, but hides herself at his approach, or covers herself with her clothes if she has to pass him. Even Pund-jel, the Australian Creator of all things, has a wife whose face he has never seen. Sometimes circumlocutory phrases are used, although, as will be seen presently, these are more usually applied to supernatural beings. For example, among the Amazulu the woman must not call her husband by name; therefore, when speaking of him, she will say, 'Father of So-andso,' meaning one of her children. As the Hindu wife is never, under any circumstances, to mention her husband's name, she calls him 'He,' 'The Master,' 'Swamy,' etc. An old-fashioned Midland cottager's wife rarely speaks of her husband by name, the pronoun 'he,' supplemented by 'my man,' or 'my master,' is sufficient distinction. Gregor says that 'in Buckie there are certain family names that fishermen will not pronounce,' the folk in the village of Coull speaking of 'spitting out the bad name.' If such a name be mentioned in their hearing, they spit, or, in- the vernacular, 'chiff,' and the man who bears the dreaded name is called a 'chifferoot.' When occasion to speak of him arises, a circumlocutory phrase is used, as. 'The man it diz so in so,' or 'The laad it lives at such and such a place.' As further showing how barbaric ideas persist in the heart of civilisation, there is an overwhelming feeling against hiring men bearing the reprobated names as hands for the boats in the herring fishing season; and when they have been hired before their names were known, their wages have been refused if the season has been a failure. 'Ye hinna hid sic a fishin' this year is ye hid the last,' said a woman to the daughter of a famous fisher. 'Na, na! faht wye cud we? We wiz in a chifferoot's 'oose, we cudnae hae a fushin'.' In some of the villages on the east coast of Aberdeenshire it was accounted unlucky to meet any one of the name of Whyte when going to sea. Lives would be lost, or the catch of fish would be poor. In the Story of Tangalimbibo ' the heroine speaks of things done 'knowingly by people whose names may not be mentioned'; upon which Mr. Theal remarks, 'no Kaffir woman may pronounce the names of any of her husband's male relatives in the ascending line; she may not even pronounce any word in which the principal syllable of his name occurs.' Some further examples of this extension of the general superstition to parts of the name will be given further on when dealing with higher principalities and powers. Meanwhile, the curious set of avoidance-customs just illustrated naturally prompt inquiry as to their origin. Upon this little, if any, light can be thrown. The relation of these customs to the general system of taboo is obvious, but what motive prompted this particular, and to us whimsical, code of etiquette, remains a problem not the less difficult of solution in the face of the wide distribution of the custom. Long before any systematic inquiry into social usages was set afoot, and before any importance was attached to the folk-tale as holding primitive ideas in solution, the taboo-incident was familiar in stories of which 'Cupid and Psyche,' and the more popular 'Beauty and the Beast,' are types. The man and woman must not see each other, or call each other by name; or, as in the Welsh and other forms of the story, the bride must not be touched with iron. But the prohibition is broken; curiosity, in revolt, from Eden onwards, against restraint, disobeys, and the unlucky wax drops on the cheek of the fair one, who thenceforth disappears. From Timbuctoo and North America, from Australia and Polynesia, and from places much nearer home than these, travellers have collected evidence of the existence of the custom on which the fate of many a wedded pair in fact and fiction hashinged. Herodotus gives us a gossipy story on this matter, which is of some value. He says that some of the old Ionian colonists brought no women with them, but took wives of the women of the Carians, whose fathers they had slain. Therefore the women made a law to themselves, and handed it down to their daughters, that they should never sit at meat with their husbands, and that none should call her husband by name. Disregarding the explanation of the formulating of social codes by women bereaved of husbands and lovers, which Herodotus, assuming this to be an isolated case, appears to suggest, we find in the reference to the abducting of the Carians an illustration of the ancient practice of obtaining wives by forcible capture, and the consequent involuntary mingling of people of alien race and speech. That, however, carries us but a little, if any, way towards explaining the avoidance-customs, the origin of which remains a perplexing problem. In an important paper on the 'Development of Institutions applied to Marriage and Descent, Professor Tylor formulated an ingenious method, the pursuit of which may help us toward a solution. He shows that the custom cannot arise from local idiosyncrasies, because in cataloguing some three hundred and fifty peoples he finds it in vogue among sixty-six peoples widely distributed over the globe; that is, he finds forty-five examples of avoidance between the husband and his wife's relations; thirteen examples between the wife and her husband's relations; and eight examples of mutual avoidance. The schedules also show a relation between the avoidance-customs and 'the customs of the world as to residence after marriage.' Among the three hundred and fifty peoples the husband goes to live with his wife's family in sixty-five instances, while there are one hundred and forty-one cases in which the wife takes up her abode with her husband's family. Thus there is a well-marked preponderance indicating that ceremonial avoidance by the husband is in some way connected with his living with his wife's family, and *vice versa* as to the wife and the husband's family. The reason of this connection 'readily presents itself, inasmuch as the ceremony of not speaking to and pretending not to see some well-known person close by, is familiar enough to ourselves in the social rite which we call "cutting." This indeed with us implies aversion, and the implication comes out even more strongly in objection to utter the name ("we never mention her," as the song has it).' It is different, however, in the barbaric custom, for here the husband is none the less on friendly terms with his wife's people because they may not take any notice of one another. As the husband has intruded himself among a family which is not his own, and into a house where he has no right, it seems not difficult to understand their marking the difference between him and themselves by treating him formally as a stranger. John Tanner, the adopted Ojibwa, describes his being taken by a friendly Assineboin into his lodge, and seeing how at his companion's entry the old father- and mother-in-law covered up their heads in their blankets till their son-in-law got into the compartment reserved for him, where his wife brought him his food. So like is the working of the human mind in all stages of civilisation that our own language conveys in a familiar idiom the train of thought which governed the behaviour of the parents of the Assineboin's wife. We have only to say that they do not recognise their son-in-law, and we shall have condensed the whole proceeding into a single word. A seemingly allied custom is that of naming the father after the child, this being found among peoples practising avoidance-customs, where a status is given to the husband only on the birth of the first child. The naming of him as father of 'So-and-so' is a recognition of paternity, and also a recognition of him by the wife's kinsfolk.

To refer to these strange and unexplained customs is to bring home the salutary fact that perchance we may never get at the back of many a seeming vagary of social life. Human institutions, like man himself, are of vast antiquity, and to project ourselves into the conditions under which some of them arose is not possible. But at least we can avoid darkening the obscure by:

'multiplying words without knowledge.'

Euphemisms and Name-Changes

Persons and things cannot remain nameless, and avoidance of one set of names compels the use of others. Hence ingenuity comes into play to devise substitutes, roundabout phrases, euphemisms, and the like. Many motives are at work in the selection. (i) Both dead and living things are often given complimentary names in 'good omen words,' as the Cantonese call them, in place of names that it is believed will grate or annoy, such mode of flattery being employed to ward off possible mischief, and also through fear of arousing jealousy or spite in maleficent spirits.(ii) Names are also changed with the object of confusing or deceiving the agents of disease, and even death itself. (iii) Certain rites, notably that of blood-brotherhood, are accompanied by exchange of names or adoption of new names; while in near connection with this is the substitution of new names for birth-names at the initiation ceremonies to which reference has been made.

i) The flattering and cajoling words in which barbaric man addresses the animals he desires to propitiate, or designs to kill, are due to belief in their kinship with him, and in the transmigration of souls which makes the beat a possible embodiment of some ancestor or another animal. Hence the homage paid to it while the man stands ready to spear or shoot it. Throughout the northern part of Eurasia, the bear has been a chief object of worship, an apologetic and propitiatory ceremonies accompany the slaying of him for food. The Amos Yezo and the Gilyaks of Eastern Siberia beg his pardon and worship his dead body, hanging up his skull on a tree as a charm against evil spirits. Swedes, Lapps, Finns, and Esthonians apply the tenderest and most coaxing terms to him. The Swedes and Lapps avert his wrath by calling him the 'old man' and 'grandfather'; the Esthon speak of him as the 'broad footed,' but it is among the Finns that we find the most euphemistic names applied to him The forty sixth rune of the *Kalevala* has for its theme the capture and killing of the 'sacred Otso,' who is also addressed as the 'honey eater,' the 'fur-robed,' the 'forest apple,' who gives his life 'a sacrifice to Northland.' When he is slain, Wäinämöinen, the old magician-hero of the story, sings the birth and fate of Otso, and artfully strives to make the dead grizzly believe that no cruel hand killed him, but that he fell

'From the fir-tree where he slumbered,
Tore his breast upon the branches,
Freely gave his life to others.'

Thorpe says that in Swedish popular belief there are certain animals which should not at any time be spoken of by their proper names, but always with kind allusions. 'If any one speaks slightingly to a cat, or beats her, her name must not be uttered, for she belongs to the hellish crew, and is intimate with the Berg-troll in the mountains, where she often goes. In speaking of the cuckoo, the owl, and the magpie, great caution is necessary, lest one should be ensnared, as they are birds of sorcery. Such birds, also snakes, one ought not to kill without cause, lest their death be avenged; and, in like manner, Mohammedan women dare not call a snake by its name lest it bite them.' The Swedes fear to tread on a toad, because it may be an enchanted princess. The fox is called 'blue-foot,' or 'he that goes in the forest'; among the Esthonians he is 'grey-coat'; and in Mecklenburg, for twelve days after Christmas, he goes by the name 'long-tail.' InSweden the seal is 'brother Lars,' and throughout Scandinavia the superstitions about wolves are numerous. In some districts during a portion of the spring the peasants dare not call that animal by his usual name, Varg, lest he carry off the cattle, so they substitute the names Ulf, Grahans, or 'gold-foot,' because in olden days, when dumb creatures spoke, the wolf said

'If thou callest me *Varg*, I will be wroth with thee,
But if thou callest me *of gold*, I will be kind to thee.'

The Claddagh folk of Gaiway would not go out to fish if they saw a fox, and the name is as unlucky as the thing. Hence Livonian fishermen (and the same superstition is prevalent from Ireland to Italy) fear to endanger the success of their nets by calling certain animals, as the hare, pig, dog, and so forth, by their common names; while the Esthonians fear to mention the hare lest their crops of flax should fail. In Annam the tiger is called 'grandfather' or 'lord'; and both in Northern Asia and Sumatra the same device of using some bamboozling name is adopted. 'Among the Jews the taboo had great force, for they were forbidden to have leaven in their houses during the Passover, and they abstained from even using the word. Being forbidden swine's flesh, they avoid the word pig altogether, and call that animal *dabchar acheer*, "the other thing." In Canton the porpoise or river-pig is looked upon as a creature of ill-omen, and on that account its name is tabooed.'

The desire not to offend, to 'let sleeping dogs lie,' as we say, explains why the Hindus call Siva, their god of destruction, the 'gracious one,' and why a like euphemism was used by the Greeks when speaking of the Furies as the Euménides. Similarly, both Greek and Gaiway peasants call the fairies 'the others,' while the natives of the Gilbert and Marshall Islands, Mr. Louis Becke tells me, speak of the spirits as 'they,' 'those,' or 'the thing.' With sly humour, not unmixed with respect for the 'quality,' the Irish speak of the tribes of the goddess Danu as 'the gentry'; in Sligo we hear of the 'royal gentry'; in Glamorganshire the fairies are called the 'mother's blessing.' If the fays are the 'good people,' the witches are 'good dames,' and their gatherings 'the sport of the good company.' It is a Swedish belief that if one speaks of the troll-pack or witch-crew, and names fire and water, or the church to which one goes (this last condition is probably post-Christian), no harm can arise. 'Even inanimate things,' Thorpe adds, 'are not at all times to be called by their usual names'; fire, for example, is on some occasions not to be called *eld* or *ell*, but *hetta* (heat); water used for brewing, not *vatu*, but *lag* or *lou*, otherwise the beer would not be so good.

The dread that praises or soft phrases may call the attention of the ever-watchful maleficent spirits to the person thus favoured, causing the evil eye to cast its baleful spell, or black magic to do its fell work, has given rise to manifold precautions. In modern Greece any allusion to the beauty or strength of the child is avoided; and if such words slip out, they are at once atoned for by one of the traditional expiatory formulas. The world-wide belief in the invisible powers as, in the main, keen to pounce on mortals, explains the Chinese custom of giving their boys a girl's name to deceive the gods; sometimes tabooing names altogether, and calling the child 'little pig' or 'little dog.' In India, especially when several male children have died in the family, boys are dressed as girls to avert further misfortune: sometimes a nose-ring is added as further device. Pausanias tells the story of the young Achilles wearing female attire and living among maidens, and to this day the peasants of Achill Island (on the north-west coast of Ireland) dress their boys as girls till they are about fourteen years old to deceive the boy seeking devil. In the west of Ireland some phrase invocative of blessing should be used on entering a cottage, or meeting a peasant, or saluting a child, because this shows that one has no connection with the fairies, and will not bring bad luck. 'Any one who did not give the usual expressions, as *Màmdeud*, "God save you"; *Slaunter*, "your good health"; and *Boluary*, "God bless the work," was looked on with suspicion.' A well-mannered Turk will not pay a compliment without uttering 'Mashallah'; an Italian will not receive one without saying the protective 'Grazia a Deó'; and the English peasant-woman has her 'Lord be wi' us' ready when flattering words are said about her babe. In each case the good power is invoked as protector against the dangers of fascination and other forms of the black art.

A survival of this feeling exists in the modern housewife's notion, that if she comments on the luck attaching to some household god, 'pride goes before a fall.' She may have exulted over the years in which a favourite china service has remained intact, and the next day, as she reaches down some of the pieces, the memory of her vaunting causes the hand to tremble, and the precious ware is smashed to atoms on the floor. It has been often remarked that if any mishaps attend a ship on her first voyage, they follow her ever after. The probable explanation is that the knowledge of the accident befalling her induces an anxious feeling on the part of those responsible for her safety, which often unnerves them in a crisis, and brings about the very calamity which they fear, and which under ordinary conditions could be averted.

Among the Hindus, when a parent has lost a child by disease, which, as is usually the case, can be attributed to fascination or other demoniacal influence, it is a common practice to call the next baby by some opprobrious name, with the intention of so depreciating it that it may be regarded as worthless, and so protected from the evil eye of the envious. Thus a male child is called Kuriya, or 'dunghill'; Khadheran or Ghasita, 'He that has been dragged along the ground'; Dukhi or Dukhita, 'The afflicted one'; Phatingua, 'grasshopper'; Jhingura, 'cricket'; Bhikra or Bhikhu, 'beggar'; Gharib, 'poor'; and so on. So a girl is called Andhri, 'blind'; Tinkouriyâ or Chhahkauriyâ, 'She that was sold for three or six cowry shells'; Dhuriyâ, 'dusty'; Machhiyâ, 'fly,' and so on. All this is connected with what the Scots call 'fore-speaking,' when praise beyond measure, praise accompanied with a sort of amazement or envy, is considered likely to be followed by disease or accident. In keeping with this is the story of the pessimist invalid who, admitting himself better to-day, added that he would not be so well to-morrow!

(ii) In barbaric belief both disease and death are due to maleficent agents, any theory of natural causes being foreign to the savage mind; hence euphemisms to avert tile evil. The Dyaks of Borneo call the smallpox 'chief' or 'jungle leaves,' or say, 'Has he left you? ' while the Cantonese speak of this 'Attila of the host of diseases' as 'heavenly flower' or 'good intention,' and deify it as a goddess. The Greeks call it Εὐλογία, or 'she that must be named with respect.' 'Similarly, the Chinese deem ague to be produced by a ghost or spirit, and for fear of offending him they will not speak of that disease under its proper name.' De Quincey has remarked on the avoidance of all mention of death as a common euphemism; and of this China is full of examples. In the *Book of Rites* it is called 'the great sickness,' and when a man dies, he is said to have 'entered the measure,' certain terms being also applied in the case of certain persons. For example, the Emperor's death is called *pang*, 'the mountain has fallen'; when a scholar dies he is *pat luk*, 'without salary or emolument.' 'Collins' are tabooed under the term 'longevity boards.' Mr. Giles says that 'boards of old age,' and 'clothes of old age sold here,' are common shop-signs in every Chinese city; death and burial being always, if possible, spoken of euphemistically in some such terms as these.

50

The belief that spirits know folks by their names further explains the barbaric attitude towards disease and death. In Borneo the name of a sick child is changed so as to confuse or deceive the spirit of the disease; the Lapps change a child's baptismal name if it falls ill, and rebaptize it at every illness, as if they thought to bamboozle the spirit by this simple stratagem of an alias. When the life of a Kwapa Indian is supposed to be in danger from illness, he at once seeks to get rid of his name, and sends to another member of the tribe, who goes to the chief and buys a new name, which is given to the patient. With the abandonment of the old name it is believed that the sickness is thrown off. 'On the reception of the new name the patient becomes related to the Kwapa who purchased it. Any Kwapa can change or abandon his personal name four times, but it is considered bad luck to attempt such a thing for the fifth time.' The Rabbis recommended the giving secretly of a new name, as a means of new life, to him who is in danger of dying. The Rev. Hilderic Friend vouches for the genuineness of the following story, the bearing of which on the continuity of barbaric and quasi-civilised ideas is significant:--'In the village of S--, near Hastings, there lived a couple who had named their first-born girl Helen. The child sickened and died, and when another daughter was born, she was named after her dead sister. But she also died, and on the birth of a third daughter the cherished name was repeated. This third Helen died, "and no wonder," the neighbours said; "it was because the parents had used the first child's name for the others." About the same time a neighbour had a daughter, who was named Marian because of her likeness to a dead sister. She showed signs of weakness soon after birth, and all said that she would die as the three Helens had died, because the name Marian ought not to have been used. It was therefore tabooed, and the girl was called Maude. She grew to womanhood, and was married; but so completely had her baptismal name of Marian been shunned, that she was married under the name of Maude, and by it continues to be known to this day.'

The Chinooks changed their names when a near relative died, in the belief that the spirits would be attracted back to earth if they heard familiar names. The Lenguas of Brazil changed their names on the death of any one, for they believed that the dead knew the names of all whom they had left behind, and might return to look for them: hence they changed their names, hoping that if the dead came back they could not find them. Although the belief, that if the dead be named their ghosts will appear, is found in this crude form only among barbaric folk, there is, in this attitude towards the unseen, no qualitative difference between savage and civilised man. Wherever there prevail anthropomorphic ideas about the Deity, i.e. conception of Him as a 'non-natural, magnified man,' to use Matthew Arnold's phrase, there necessarily follows the assumption that the relations between God and man are, essentially, like in character to those subsisting between human beings. The majority of civilised mankind have no doubt that God knows each one of them and all their belongings by name, as He is recorded to have known men of olden time, addressing them direct or through angels by their names, and sometimes altering these. Take for example: 'Neither shall thy name any more be called Abram, but thy name shall be Abraham, for a father of many nations have I made thee' (Genesis xvii. 5). 'And he said, Thy name shall be called no more Jacob, but Israel, for as a prince hast thou power with God and with men, and hast prevailed' (ibid. xxxii. ~28). 'And the Lord said unto Moses, I will do this thing also that thou hast spoken; for thou hast found grace in My sight, and I know thee by name' (Exodus xxxiii. 17).

Miscellaneous as are the contents of the Old and New Testaments, the relations between the several parts of which have arisen, in many instances, through the arbitrary decisions of successive framers of the canon, the belief in the efficacy of names, and in their integral connection with things, runs through the Bible, because that belief is involved in the unscientific theories of phenomena which are present in all ancient literatures. Man may soar into the abstract, but he has to live in the concrete. When he descends from hazy altitudes to confront the forms in which he envisages his ideas, he finds what slight advance he has made upon primitive conceptions. The God of the current theology is no nameless Being, and one of the prominent members of the spiritual hierarchy is that Recording Angel who writes the names of redeemed mortals in the Book of Life. Amidst all the vagueness which attaches itself to conceptions of another world, there is the feeling that the names of the departed are essential to their identification when they enter the unseen, and to their recognition by those who will follow them. Civilised and savage are here on the same intellectual plane.

To name the invisible is to invoke its presence or the manifestation of its power. The Norse witches tied up wind and foul matter in a bag, and then, undoing the knot, shouted 'Wind, in the devil's name,' when the hurricane swept over land and sea; the witch's dance could be stopped, and the dancers dispersed, by uttering the name of God or Christ; and the like idea is expressed in the phrase, 'Talk of the devil, and you will see his horns.'

(iii) In Grimms story of the 'Goose Girl,' when the old queen's daughter starts for the kingdom of her betrothed, her mother gives her costly trinkets, Cups and jewels of gold, and, taking a handkerchief, cuts her own finger till it bleeds, letting three drops of blood fall on the handkerchief. This she gives to the princess, bidding her preserve it, because she will need it on the way. After she and her waiting-maid had ridden some miles, a great thirst fell upon her, and she bade the girl dismount to fill the golden cup with water from a stream hard by. But the girl refused, whereupon the princess alighted to slake her thirst, using only her hands, because the girl would not let her have the cup. As she drank she sighed, and the three drops of blood said, 'If thy mother knew this, her heart would break.' The princess mounted her horse, but had not gone far before her thirst returned; again the maid refused to serve her, and again she alighted to drink. But this time, as she stooped to the stream, her handkerchief fell out of her bosom, and was carried away by the current. Thenceforth her strength left her, and the maid had her wholly in her power. She made the princess exchange clothes and horses, and then, when the palace was reached, forbade her entrance, while she, pretending to be the expected bride, went in, and was embraced by the prince. Of course, as usual in fiction, all came right in the end; but we are not further concerned with the fortunes of the 'persons, the story, one of a group of kindred folk-tales, being cited only to show how the main incident revolves on the barbaric belief in the efficacy of blood.

In the early stages of society, blood-relationship is the sole tie that unites men into tribal communities. As Sir Henry Maine has observed, 'there was no brotherhood recognised by our savage forefathers except actual consanguinity regarded as a fact. If a man was not of kin to another, there was nothing between them. He was an enemy to be slain or spoiled or hated, as much as the wild beasts upon which the tribes made war, as belonging indeed to the craftiest and the cruelest order of white animals. It would scarcely be too strong an assertion that the dogs which followed the camp had more in common with it than the tribesmen of an alien and unrelated tribe.' And although enlarged knowledge, in unison with growing recognition of mutual rights and obligations, has extended the feeling of community, an unprejudiced outlook on the world does not warrant the hope that the old tribal feeling has passed the limits of race. Human nature being what it is, charged with the manifold forces of self-assertion and aggression bequeathed by a stormy and struggling past, the various nationalities, basing their claims and their unity on the theory of blood-relationship, do their best to dispel the dream of the unity of all mankind.

As already observed, the importance and sanctity attached to blood explain the existence of a large number of rites connected with covenants between man and his fellows, and between man and his gods; covenants sealed by the drinking, or interfusing, or offering of blood. Any full account of these rites, notably on their sacrificial side, would need a volume, but here reference is again made to them in connection with the exchange of names, or with the bestowal of new names, which sometimes accompanies them.

Mr. Herbert Spencer remarks, that 'by absorbing each other's blood, men are supposed to establish actual community of nature'; and as it is a widely diffused belief that the name is vitally connected with its owner, 'to exchange names is to establish some participation in one another's being.' Hence the blending is regarded as more complete when exchange of name goes with the mingling of blood, making even more obligatory the rendering of services between those who are no longer aliens to each other. When Tolo, a Shastikan chief, made a treaty with Colonel M'Kee, an American officer, as to certain concessions, he desired some ceremony of brotherhood to make the covenant binding, and, after some parleying, proposed an exchange of names, which was agreed to. Thenceforth he became M'Kee, and M'Kee became Tolo. But after a while the Indian found that the American was shuffling over the bargain, whereupon 'M'Kee angrily cast off that name, and refused to resume that of Tolo.' He would not answer to either, and to the day of his death insisted that his name, and, therefore, his identity, was lost. There is no small pathos in this revolt of the rude moral sense of the Indian against the white man's trickery, and in the utter muddle of his mind as to who and what he had become.

The custom of name-exchanging existed in the West Indies at the time of Columbus; and in the South Seas, Captain Cook and a native, named Oree, made the exchange, whereby Cook became Oree and the native became Cookee. 'But Cadwallader Colden's account of his new name is admirable evidence of what there is in a name to the mind of the savage. "The first time I was among the *Mohawks* I had this compliment from one of their old *Sachems*, which he did by giving me his own name, *Cayenderongue*. He had been a notable warrior, and he told me that now I had a right to assume all the acts of valour he had performed, and that now my name would echo from hill to hill over all the Five Nations." When Colden went back into the same part ten or twelve years later, he found that he was still known by the name he had thus received, and that the old chief had taken another.'

In the manhood-initiation rites of the native Australians a long series of ceremonies is followed by the conferring of a new name on the youth, and the sponsor, who may be said to correspond to a godfather among ourselves, opens a vein in his own arm, and the lad then drinks the warm blood. A curious addition to the New South Wales ritual consists in the giving of a white stone or quartz crystal, called *mundie*, to the novitiate in manhood when he receives his new name. 'This stone is counted a gift from deity, and is held peculiarly sacred. A test of the young man's moral stamina is made by the old men trying, by all sorts of persuasion, to induce him to surrender this possession when first he has received it. This accompaniment of a new name is worn concealed in the hair, tied up in a packet, and is never shown to the women, who are forbidden to look at it under pain of death.'

TABOO ON NAMES OF KINGS AND PRIESTS

Avoidance and veneration superstitions gather force with the ascending rank of individuals. The divinity that 'doth hedge' both king and priest, which two offices were originally blended in one man, increases the power of the taboo. Until Mr. Frazer published his *Golden Bough*, the significance of this taboo, as applied to royal and sacerdotal persons, was somewhat obscure. But the large, indeed overcrowding, array of examples which his industry has collected and his ingenuity interpreted, make it clear that the priest-king was regarded as the incarnation of supernatural powers on whose unhindered and effective working the welfare of men depended. That being the belief, obviously the utmost care was used to protect in every possible way the individual in whom those powers were incarnated. As the *Golden Bough* does not come under the head of popular books in the sense of being widely read, although, within a limited circle, often quoted, it may be well to explain this barbaric theory of the spirit indwelling in man by citing the typical example which Mr. Frazer has chosen, and which gives its title to his book.

Three miles from Aricia, an old town on the Alban Hills, a few miles from Rome, there was a famous grove and temple dedicated to Diana. The temple was on the northern shore of the lake under the cliffs on which the modern village of Nemi stands. The priest of that temple, which was held in high repute throughout Italy, was called Rex Nemorensis, or 'King of the Grove,' and, at least in later times, he was always a runaway slave. The strangest feature of the business was that he must be a murderer, because he could obtain the priestly office only by killing the man who held it, and, therefore, when he had secured it, he had to be always on the alert against being attacked. Lord Macaulay, in his poem of the 'Battle of Lake Regillus' (*Lays of Ancient Rome*), refers to this curious custom

'From the still, glassy lake that sleeps
Beneath Aricia's trees--
Those trees in whose dim shadow
The ghostly priest doth reign,
The priest who slew the slayer,
And shall himself be slain.'

This priest-king kept special guard over a sacred tree, and if any runaway slave could succeed in breaking-off a branch from it, the priest was compelled to fight him in single combat. The existence of this custom within historical times is proved by the circumstance that the Emperor Caligula gave orders that the Rex Nemorensis, who during his reign had long been left unassailed, should be attacked and killed. But its origin and reason had then become forgotten, and it is only in our time that its connection with the groups of rites and ceremonies gathering round certain phases of nature-worship, notably tree-worship, has been established. In the general application of the barbaric conception of life indwelling in all things, and especially active where motion was apparent, and where growth, maturity, and decline marked the object, the tree was believed to be the abode of a spirit, while the priest was regarded as an incarnation of the tree-spirit on which the fruitfulness of the soil depended. We have seen how universal is the barbaric belief in real and vital connection between one living thing and another, and also between one non-living thing and another; and it is therein that the key is found to the belief that if the Rex Nemorensis was suffered to live on until he became decrepit by age, then the earth would become old and feeble also, the trees yielding no fruit and the fields no harvest. Therefore, to prevent this, the priest-king, as an incarnated god, was not allowed to reach old age; and when his waning strength was proved by his inability to hold his own against the aggressor, he was killed, and the divine spirit, with its power and vigour unimpaired, was believed to pass into his slayer and successor. The sacred tree, it may be added, from which the runaway slave sought to break off the 'Golden Bough '--the parasitic mistletoe, Mr. Frazer suggests--was probably an oak, the worship of which was general among the Aryan-speaking peoples of Europe. Tradition averred that the fateful branch which Aeneas plucked at the sibyl's bidding, before he essayed the perilous journey to the underworld, was the Golden Bough.

Incarnate gods are common enough in rude society, the incarnation being sometimes temporary, and sometimes permanent. The Cantonese apply the expressive term 'god boxes' to priests in whom the gods are believed to dwell from time to time; but in seeking for correspondences to the Rex Nemorensis, we find corroborative examples in old-world traditions, and among savage races of to-day. Among the former, we have those relating to the Mikado, who, although now somewhat shorn of his ancient glory, and stripped of the mystery that invested him, was regarded as an incarnation of the sun, all the gods repairing once every year to spend a month at his court. He was required to take rigorous care of his person, and 'to do such things as, examined according to the custom of other nations, would be thought ridiculous and impertinent.' Like the high pontiff of the Zapotecs in South Mexico, his feet must never touch the ground; the sun must never shine on his naked head; he was required to sit motionless all the day so that tranquillity might be assured to his empire; and such holiness was ascribed to all the parts of his body, that 'he dare not cut off' neither his hair, nor his beard, nor his nails.' But 'that he might not grow too dirty, he was washed in his sleep, because a theft at such time did not prejudice his holiness or dignity.' The pots in which his food was cooked and served were destroyed lest they should fall into lay hands; his clothes were fatal to those who touched them--for taboo is extended from the tabooed person to the things he wears, or tastes, or handles, even to the objects on which he looks, as illustrated by the Samoan high priest and prophet Tupai. 'His very glance was poison. If he looked at a coco-nut tree it died, and if he glanced at a bread-fruit tree it also withered away. In Tahiti, if a chief's foot touches the earth, the spot which it touches becomes taboo thenceforth, and none may approach it; chiefs are therefore carried in Tahiti when they go out. If he enters a house it becomes taboo; and in ancient Greece the priest and priestess of Artemis Hymnia amongst the Orchomenians, and the Rechabites among the Jews, might not enter a private house, 'for the same reason as the Polynesian chief,' as Dr. Jevons correctly suggests. As with the Caesars, the Pharaohs were deified in their lifetime, and their daily routine was regulated after the fashion of the Mikado, while they too were held blamable if the crops failed.

Returning to Rome, we find the Flamen Dialis, who was consecrated to the service of Jupiter, and who, therefore, was probably the incarnated sky-spirit, tied and bound by rules governing the minutest details of his life. He might not ride or even touch ~a horse, nor see an army under arms, nor wear a ring which was not broken, nor have a knot in any part of his garments; no fire except a sacred fire might be taken out of his house; he might not touch wheaten flour or leavened bread; he might not touch or even name a goat, a dog, raw meat, beans, and ivy; he might not walk under a vine; the feet of his bed had to be daubed with mud, and iron was put at the head of it as a charm against evil spirits; his hair could be cut only by a free man and with a bronze knife, and his hair and nails, when cut, had to be buried under a lucky tree; he might not touch a dead body, nor enter a place where one was burned; he might not see work being done on holy days; he might not be uncovered 'or annoint himselfe' in the open air; if a man in bonds were taken into his house he had to be unbound, and the cords had to be drawn up through a hole in the roof, and so let down into the street. His wife, the Flaminica, had to observe nearly the same rules, and others of her own besides, and when she died the 'Flamen or Priest of Jupiter had to give up his Priesthood or Sacerdotall dignitie.' Plutarch was greatly puzzled in his search after a rational explanation of these and kindred matters, and he has many a fanciful comment upon them, erroneous as well as fanciful, because it did not occur to him that the explanation must be sought in the persistence of the barbaric ideas of remote ancestors. This perception of continuity, illuminated by numerous examples at home and abroad, is wholly modern, and therefore, after tracking the vitality of a belief or custom among the illiterate in civilised communities, we cross the seas in search of parallels among barbaric folk. In Lower Guinea, the priest-king, who was a wind-god, was not allowed to quit his chair to sleep, because if he lay down no wind could arise; while in Congo it was held that if the incarnated priest-king died a natural death, the world would perish. Therefore, like the Rex Nemorensis, he had to be kept in vigour at the risk of his life, 'worshipped as a god one day, and killed as a criminal the next.' As these wind and weather gods are held responsible for droughts and bad harvests, it is not surprising that there is no rush of candidates for vacant thrones with their miserable restraints and isolation, and that the tactics of the press-gang have sometimes to be resorted to in order that the succession of the incarnated may not be broken.

In this group of customs hedging in the royal person and his belongings there lie the materials out of which has been evolved the well-nigh obsolete and long mischievous theory of the right divine of kings, with its resulting belief in their possession of powers bordering on the supernatural, as in the curing of scrofula by their touch. When Charles I. visited Scotland in 1633, he is said to have 'heallit one hundred persons of the cruelles or Kings eivell, young and olde,' in Holyrood Chapel on St. John's day; and, although William III. had the good sense to pooh-pooh it, it was not until the reign of George I. that the custom was abolished.

The intangible, even more than the tangible, would be the subject of taboo, as coming near the confines of that spiritual realm where man had no control. Hence the secrecy which hedged the royal name; a feature which Mr. Frazer omits from his otherwise comprehensive survey.

In China the *ming* or proper name of the reigning Emperor (sight of whom is tabooed when he appears in public, even his guards having to turn their back to the line when the Son of Heaven approaches) is sacred, and must be spelt differently during his lifetime. Although given in the prayer offered at the imperial worship of ancestors, it is not permitted to be written or pronounced by any subject. 'The first month of the Chinese year is called *Ching-ut*. The word ching in this particular case is pronounced in the first tone or "upper monotone," though it really belongs to the third or "upper falling tone." A Chinese work explains this as follows:

There lived in the third century c.e. a noted Emperor who assumed the title of *She Hwang-Ti*. He succeeded to the throne of China (T'sin) at the age of thirteen, and, following up the career of conquest initiated by his tutor, he was able to found a new empire on the ruins of the Chinese feudal system, and in the twenty-sixth year of his reign declared himself sole master of the Chinese Empire. He was superstitious, and his desire to be considered great shows itself in the manner in which he destroyed the classics of his land, that his name might be handed down to posterity as the first Emperor of China. His name was *Ching*, and, that it might be ever held sacred, he commanded that the syllable *ching* be tabooed. Hence the change in pronunciation referred to.' No Korean dare utter his king's name. When the king dies he is given another name, by which his royal personality may be kept clear in the mass of names that fill history. But his real name, the name he bears in life, is never spoken save in the secrecy of the palace harem. And even there it is spoken only by the privileged lips of his favourite wife and his most spoiled children. Polack says that from a New Zealand chief being called 'Wai,' which means 'water,' a new name had to be given to water. A chief was called 'Maripi,' or 'knife,' and knives were therefore called by another name, 'nekra.' In Tahiti, when a chief took highest rank, any words resembling his name were changed: 'even to call a horse or dog "prince" or "princess" was disgusting to the native mind.'

The custom is known as *te pi*, and, in the case of a king whose name was Tu, all words in which that syllable occurred were changed: for example, *fetu*, star, becoming *fetia*; or *tui*, to strike, being changed to *tiai*. Vancouver observes that at the accession of that ruler, which took place between his own visit and that of Captain Cook, no less than forty or fifty of the names most in daily use had been entirely changed. As Professor Max Muller ingeniously remarks, 'It is as if with the accession of Queen Victoria, either the word Victory had been tabooed altogether, or only part of it, as tori, so as to make it high treason to speak of Tories during her reign.' On his accession to royalty, the name of the king of the Society Islands was changed, and any one uttering the old name was put to death with all his relatives. Death was the penalty for uttering the name of the king of Dahomey in his presence; his name was, indeed, kept secret lest the knowledge of it should enable any enemy to harm him; hence the names by which the different kings have been known to Europeans are aliases--in native term, 'strong names.' The London newspapers of June 1890 reprinted extracts from a letter in the *Vossische Zeitung* relating the adventures of Dr. Bayol, Governor of Kotenon, who had been imprisoned by the King of Dahomey. The king was too suspicious to sign the letter written in his name to the President of the French Republic, probably through fear that M. Carnot might bewitch him through it. An interesting comment on the foregoing examples is supplied by a painting on the temple of Rameses II. at Gurnah, whereon Trim, Safekht, and Thoth are depicted as inscribing that monarch's name on the sacred tree of Heliopolis, by which act he was endowed with eternal life.

The separation of the priestly and kingly offices, which followed the gradual subdivision of functions in society, tended to increase the power of the priest in the degree that he represented the kingdom of the invisible and the dreaded, and held the keys of admission therein. The king, who reigned by the grace of God, as the term goes in civilised communities, was consecrated to his office by the minister of God, and, hence, there could not fail to arise the conflicts between the temporal and the spiritual dignities of which history tells, a modern example of these being the relations between the Quirinal and the Vatican. The prerogatives which the Church claimed could only be granted by the State consenting to accept a position of vassalage illustrated by the submission of Henry iv. in the courtyard of Gregory vii. at Canossa. Whatever appertained to the sacerdotal office reflected the supreme importance of its functions; the priest, as incarnation of the god, transferred into his own person that which had secured sanctity and supremacy to the priest-king, and the king was so much the poorer. The supernatural power which the priest claimed tended to isolate him more and more from his fellows, and place him in the highest caste, whose resulting conservatism and opposition to all challenge of its claims have been among the chief arresting forces in human progress. For to admit that these claims were open to question would have been fatal to the existence of the priestly order. The taboos guarding and regulating the life of the priest-king therefore increase in rigidity when applied to priest and shrine; and how persistent they are is seen in the feeling amongst the highest races that the maltreating or killing of a priest is a greater crime than the maltreating or killing of a layman, and that the robbery of a church is a greater offence than the devouring of widows' houses.

These remarks are designed to show that the examples of royal and sacerdotal taboos cited above have increased force when applied to priests in their ascending degrees from medicine-men to popes; and perhaps one of the most striking illustrations of this is supplied by the record of customs attaching to the holy and hidden name of the priests of Eleusis. A brief account of this may close the references to name-avoidance and name-substitution so far as the living are concerned.

Some years ago a statue of one of these hierophants was found in that ancient seat of 'the Venerable Mysteries of Demeter, the most solemn rites of the Pagan world.' The inscription on its base ran thus: 'Ask not my name, the mystic rule (or packet) has carried it away into the blue sea. But when I reach the fated day, and go to the abode of the blest, then all who care for me will pronounce it.' When the priest was dead, his sons added some words, of which only a few are decipherable, the rest being mutilated. 'Now we, his children, reveal the name of the best of fathers, which, when alive, he hid in the depths of the sea. This is the famous Apollonius. . .'

The name which the priest thus desired should be kept secret until his death was the holy name--usually that of some god--which he adopted on taking his sacred office. Directly he assumed that name, it was probably written on a tablet, so that, as symbol of its secrecy, it might be buried in the depths of the sea; but when he went 'to the abode of the blest,' it was 'pronounced,' and became the name by which he was known to posterity. Some interesting questions arise out of the ceremonies attaching to the name-concealment. Among these, the chief one is the committal to the sea, which is probably connected with lustration rites; a connection further evidenced by the choice of salt instead of fresh water. The custom of sending diseases and demons out to sea in canoes or in toy-ships, is not unknown in Malaysia and other parts; but discussion on modes of transfer and expulsion of evils would lead us too far afield, and it suffices to say that, in this custom of the Greek priesthood, there was a survival of the barbaric taboo which conceals an individual's name for the same reason that it burns or buries his material belongings.

(c) TABOO ON NAMES OF THE DEAD

Passing from the living to the dead, and to *spiritual beings generally*, we find the power of taboo increased in the degree that it invests things more mysterious. The conflicting behaviour of the barbaric mind towards ghosts and all their kin should be a warning to the framers of cut-and-dried theories of the origin of religion, since no one key fits the complex wards of the lock opening the door of the unseen. Sometimes the spirits of the dead are tempted by offerings at the graves; holes are cut in the rude stone tombs to let them out, or to pass-in food to them; at other times, all sorts of devices are adopted to prevent them from finding their way back to their old haunts, the one object being to 'lay the ghost.' While memory of them abides, a large number receive a vague sort of worship in which fear is the chief element, only a few securing such renown as obtains their promotion to the rank of godlings, and, by another step or two, of gods. Others there are for whom no hope of deification removes the terrors of the underworld; while the remainder, in their choice of evils, would accept the cheerless Hades so that they might not wander as unburied shades. All which is bewildering enough and fatal to any uniformity of principle ruling conceptions of another life, but not less bewildering than the result of any attempt to extract from intelligent people who believe in a future state some coherent idea of what happens to the soul between death and the day of judgment. Vague and contradictory as both savage and civilised notions on these matters may be, there is, nevertheless, at the base a common feeling that prompts to awe and hushed tone when speaking of the dead. To quote from Mrs. Barrett Browning's 'Cowper's Grave,' he is 'Named softly as the household name of one whom God hath taken.'

Among a large number of barbaric races he is never named, because to do so is to disturb him or to summon him, and that is the last thing desired. When any member of a tribe died, the Tasmanians abstained ever after from mentioning his name, believing that to do so would bring dire calamities upon them. In referring to such an one, they would use great circumlocution; for example, 'if William and Mary, husband and wife, were both dead, and Lucy, the deceased sister of William, had been married to Isaac, also dead, whose son Jemmy still survived, and they wished to speak of Mary,' they would say, 'the wife of the brother of Jemmy's father's wife.' So great was their fear of offending the shade of the dead by naming him, that they took every precaution to avoid being drawn into talk about him with white men. And that reluctance was extended to the absent, Backhouse recording that one of the women threw sticks at J. Thornton on his mentioning her son, who was at school at Newtown. The Tasmanian circumlocution is equalled by that of the Australian native from which Dr. Lang tried to learn the name of a slain relative. 'He told me who the lad's father was, who was his brother, what he was like, how he walked, how he held his tomahawk in his left hand instead of his right, and who were his companions; but the dreaded name never escaped his lips, and, I believe, no promises or threats could have induced him to utter it.' Lumholtz
remarks that none of the Australian aborigines 'utter the names of the dead, lest their spirits should hear the voices of the living, and thus discover their whereabouts'; and Sir George/ Grey says that the only modification of the taboo which he found among them was a lessened reluctance to utter the name of any one who had been dead for some time. In this they differ from some folk nearer home, for the Shetland Island widow cannot be got to mention the name of her husband, although she will talk of him by the hour. No dead person must be mentioned, 'for his ghost will come to him who speaks his name.' Dorman gives a touching illustration of this superstition in the Shawnee myth of Yellow Sky. She was a daughter of the tribe, and had dreams which told her that she was created for an unheard-of mission. There was a mystery about her being, and none could comprehend the meaning of her evening songs. The paths leading to her father's lodge were more beaten than those to any other. On one condition alone at last she consented to become a wife, namely, that he who wedded her should never mention her name. If he did, she warned him, a sad calamity would befall him, and he would for ever thereafter regret his thoughtlessness. After a time Yellow Sky sickened and died, and her last words were that her husband might never breathe her name. For five summers he lived in solitude, but one day, as he was by the grave of his dead wife, an Indian asked him whose it was, and in forgetfulness he uttered the forbidden name. He fell to the earth in great pain, and as darkness settled round about him a change came over him. Next morning, near the grave of Yellow Sky, a large buck was quietly feeding. It was the unhappy husband. Conversely, in Swedish folk-lore, the story is told of a bridegroom and his

friends who were riding through a wood, when they were all transformed into wolves by evil spirits. After the lapse of years, the forlorn bride was walking one day in the same forest, and in anguish of heart, as she thought of her lost lover, she shrieked out his name. Immediately he appeared in human form and rushed into her arms. The sound of his Christian name had dissolved the devilish spell that bound him. Among both the Chinook Indians and the Lenguas of Brazil, the near relatives of the deceased changed their names, lest the spirit should be drawn back to earth by hearing the old name used; while in another tribe, 'if one calls the dead by name, he must answer to the dead man's relatives. He must surrender his own blood, or pay blood-money in restitution of the life of the dead taken by him.' The Abipones invented new words for anything whose name recalled the dead person's memory, while to utter his name was a nefarious proceeding; and among certain northern tribes, when a death occurred, if a relative of the deceased was absent, his friends would hang along the road by which he would return to apprise him of the fact, so that he might not mention the dreaded name on his arrival. Among the Connecticut tribes, if the offence of naming the dead was twice repeated, death was not regarded as a punishment too severe. In 1655, Philip, having heard that another Indian had spoken the name of his deceased relative, came to the island of Nantucket to kill him, and the English had to interfere to prevent it. If among the Californian tribes the name of the dead was accidentally mentioned, a shudder passed over those present. An aged Indian of Lake Michigan explained why tales of the spirits were told only in winter, by saying that when the deep snow is on the ground the voices of those who repeat their names are muffled, but that in summer the slightest mention of them must be avoided, lest in the clear air they hear their own names and are offended. Among the Fuegians, when a child asks for its dead father or mother, it will be reproved and told not to 'speak bad words'; and the Abipones, to whom reference has just been made, will use some periphrasis for the dead, as 'the man who does not now exist.' My friend Louis Becke tells me that 'in the olden days in the Ellice Islands, it was customary to always speak of a dead man by some other name than that which he had borne when au For instance, if Kino, who in life was a builder of canoes, died, he would perhaps be spoken of "teaura moli," *i.e.* "perfectly fitting outrigger" to denote that he had been especially skilled building and fitting an outrigger to a canoe. He would never be spoken of as Kino, though his son or grandson might bear his name hereditarily.' As bearing on this last remark, among the Iroquois, the name of a dead man could not used again in the lifetime of his oldest surviving son without the consent of the latter.

To this list might be added examples like name-avoidance of the dead among Ostiaks, Ainos, Samoyeds, Papuans, Masai, and numerous other peoples at corresponding low levels culture, but that addition would only lend superfluous strength to world-wide evidence of a practice whose motive is clear, and whose interest for us chiefly lies in its witness to the like attitude of the human mind before the mystery of the hereafter.

(d) TABOO ON THE NAMES OF GODS

As with names of the lesser hierarchy of spirits, so with the name of a god; but with the added significance which deity imports. To know it, is to enable the utterer to invoke him. Moreover, it enables the human to enter into close communion with the divine, even to obtain power over the god himself. Hence the refusal of the god to tell his name, and of the devices employed to discover it. On the other hand, the feeling that the god is jealous of his name, and full of threatenings against those who take it in vain, gives rise to the employment of some other name. But, whatever may be the attitude of the worshipper, there is belief in the power of the name, and in virtues inhering therein. The gods whom man worships with bloody rites are made in his own image, and the names given them which he dreads to pronounce are his own coinage. But the lapse of time, ever investing with mystery that which is withdrawn or receding, and the stupendous force of tradition, which transmutes the ordinary into the exceptional, explain the paradox. And an of the confusion between persons and things supplies such illustration of the vagaries human mind at the barbaric stage that to look for logical sequence in its behaviour. Even where we might feel warranted in expecting a certain consistency, or a certain perception of fundamental differences, we insight lacking. Here, too, tradition power; we see how superficial are the changes in human nature as a whole, and in what small degree the 'old Adam' has been cast striking illustration of the belief in the power over the god which mortals may secure by knowledge of his name is supplied by the concealment of the name of the tutelary deity Plutarch asks, 'How commeth it to passé, that it is expressly forbidden at Rome, either to name or to demand ought as touching the god, who hath in particular recommendation and patronage the safetie and preservation of the citie; nor so much as to enquire whether the said deitie be male or female? And versely this prohibition proceedeth from a superstitious feare that they have, for that they say, that Valerius Soranus died an ill death because he presumed to utter and publish so much.' Plutarch's answer shows more approach to the true explanation than is his wont. He continues the interrogative strain: 'Is it in regard of a certaine reason that some Latin historians do allege; namely, that there be certaine evocations and enchantings of the gods by spels and charmes, through the power whereof they are of opinion that they might be able to call forth and draw away the Tutelar gods of their enemies, and to cause them to come and dwell with them; and therefore the Romans be afraid lest they may do as much for them? For, like as in times past the Tyrians, as we find upon record, when their citie was besieged, enchained the images of their gods to their shrines, for feare they would abandon their citie and be gone, and as others demanded pledges and sureties that they should come againe to their place, whensoever they sent them to any bath to be washed, or let them go to any expiation to be cleansed; even so the Romans thought, that to be altogether unknowen and not once named, was the best meanes, and surest way to keepe with their Tutelar god.' Pliny says that Verrius Flaccus quotes authors, whom he thinks trustworthy, to the effect that when the Romans laid siege to a town, the first step was for the priests to summon the guardian god of the place, and to offer him the same or a greater place in the Roman pantheon. This practice, Pliny adds, still remains in the pontifical discipline, and it is certainly for this reason that it has been kept secret under the protection of what god Rome itself has been, lest its enemies should use like tactics.

The greater gods of the Roman pantheon were of foreign origin; the religion of the Romans was wholly designed for use in practical life, and the gods who ruled human affairs in minutest detail from the hour of birth to that of death and burial were shapeless abstractions. Cunina was the guardian spirit of the cradle; Rumina, the spirit of suckling. Educa and Potina, the spirits of eating and drinking, watched over the child at home; Abeona and Iterduca, the spirits of departing and travelling, attended him on his journey; Adeona and Domiduca, the spirits of approaching and arrival, brought him home again. The threshold, the door, and the hinges each had its attendant spirit, Limertinus, Forculus, and Cardea; while Janus presided over door-openings, guarding the household from evil spirits. Agriculture being the main occupation, there were spirits of harrowing, ploughing, sowing, harvesting, and threshing; while Pecunia, the spirit of money, attended the trader, and Portunus, the harbour-spirit, guided the merchant vessel safe to port. These vague *numina* are known as 'Di Indigetes,' and it was part of the duty of the pontiffs to keep a complete register of them on lists called *indigitamenta*. Our interest here lies in the fact that they show how little, if at all, the Roman was above the savage, because he believed that it was sufficient to utter the names of any one of the 'Di Indigetes' to secure its presence and protection. Hence the importance of omitting the name of no spirit from the pontifical lists. Among the Penitential Psalms of the Babylonian scriptures, which, in the opinion of Professor Sayce, date from Accadian times, and which, in their depth of feeling and dignity, bear comparison with the Psalms of the Hebrews, we find the worshipper pleading--

'How long, O god, whom I know, and know not, shall
the fierceness of thy heart continue?

How long, O goddess, whom I know, and know not,
shall thy heart in its hostility be (not) appeased?

Mankind is made to wander, and there is none that knoweth;
Mankind, as many as pronounce a name, what do they know?'

Upon which Professor Sayce remarks: 'The belief in the mysterious power of names is still strong upon him. In fear lest the deity he has offended should not be named at all, or else be named incorrectly, he does not venture to enumerate the gods, but classes them under the comprehensive titles of the divinities with whose names he is acquainted, and of those of whose names he is ignorant. It is the same when he refers to the human race. Here, again, the ancient superstition about words shows itself plainly. If he alludes to mankind, it is to "mankind as many as pronounce a name," as many, that is, as have names which may be pronounced.'

The modern worshipper is nearer to the ancient Roman and Chaldean, and to the barbarian of past and present time, than he suspects. Every religious assembly--.for even sects who, like the Quakers, eschew all ritual, break the silence of their gatherings when the 'spirit moveth '--invokes the Deity in the feeling that thereby His nearer presence is the more assured. So that the line between the lower and the higher civilisation is hard to draw in this matter. And although undue stress might be laid on certain passages in the Bible which convey the idea of the integral relation between the Deity and His name, it is not to be questioned that the efficacy of certain rites, notably that of baptism and of exorcism, or the casting-out of demons, would be doubted if the name of the Deity was omitted.

That the gods of the higher religions, or their representatives, are described as reluctant to tell their names, and as yielding only through strategy or cunning, is in keeping with barbaric conceptions. In the Book of Judges we read that 'Manoah said unto the angel of the Lord, What is thy name, that when thy sayings come to pass we may do thee honour? And the angel of the Lord said unto him, Why askest thou thus after my name, seeing it is secret?' (or wonderful, as in the margin of the Authorised Version). A Turin papyrus, dating from the twentieth dynasty, preserves a remarkable legend of the great Râ, oldest of the gods, and one who, ruling over men as the first king- of Egypt, is depicted as in familiar converse with them. The dignity of the story, Englished by Dr. Wallis Budge, demands that it be given with only the slightest abridgement.

Now Isis was a woman who possessed words of power; her heart was wearied with the millions of men, and she chose the millions of the gods, but she esteemed more highly the millions of the *khus*. And she meditated in her heart, saying, 'Cannot I by means of the sacred name of God make myself mistress of the earth and become a goddess like unto Rd in heaven and upon earth?' Now, behold, each day Râ entered at the head of his holy mariners and established himself upon the throne of the two horizons. The holy one had grown old, he dribbled at the mouth, his spittle fell upon the earth, and his slobbering dropped upon the ground. And Isis kneaded it with earth in her hand, and formed thereof a sacred serpent in the form of a spear; she set it not upright before her face, but let it lie upon the ground in the path whereby the great god went forth, according to his heart's desire, into his double kingdom. Now the holy god arose, and the gods who followed him as though he were Pharaoh went with him; and he came forth according to his daily wont; and the sacred serpent bit him. The flame of life departed from him, and he who dwelt among the Cedars (?) was overcome. The holy god opened his mouth, and the cry of his majesty reached unto heaven. His company of gods said, 'What hath happened?' and his gods exclaimed, 'What is it?' But Râ could not answer, for his jaws trembled and all his members quaked; the poison spread swiftly through his flesh just as the Nile invadeth all his land. When the great god had stablished his heart, he cried unto those who were in his train, saying, 'Come unto me, O ye who have come into being from my body, ye gods who have come forth from me, make ye known unto Khepera that a dire calamity hath fallen upon me. My heart perceiveth it, but my eyes see it not; my hand hath not caused it, nor do I know who hath done this unto me. Never have I felt such pain, neither can sickness cause more woe than this. I am a prince, the son of a prince, a sacred essence which hath proceeded from God. I am a great one, the son of a great one, and my father planned my name; I have multitudes of names and multitudes of forms, and my existence is in every god. I have been proclaimed by the heralds Imu and Horus, and my father and my mother uttered my name; but it hath been hidden within me by him that begat me, who would not that the words of power of any seer should have dominion over me. I came forth to look upon that which I had made, I was passing through the world which I had created, when lo! something stung me, but what I know not. Is it fire? Is it water? My heart is on fire, my flesh quaketh, and trembling hath seized all my limbs. Let there be brought unto me the children of the gods with healing words and with lips that know, and with power which reacheth unto heaven.'

The children of every god came unto him in tears, Isis came with her healing words, and her mouth full of the breath of life, with her enchantments which destroy sickness, and with her words of power which make the dead to live. And she spake, saying, 'What hath come to pass, O holy father? What hath happened? A serpent hath bitten thee, and a thing which thou hast created bath lifted up his head against thee. Verily it shall be cast forth by my healing words of power, and I will drive it away from before the sight of thy sunbeams.' The holy god opened his mouth and said, 'I was passing along my path, and I was going through the two regions of my lands according to my heart's desire, to see that which I had created, when lo! I was bitten by a serpent which I saw not. Is it fire? Is it water? I am colder than water, I am hotter than fire. All my flesh sweateth, I quake, my eye hath no strength, I cannot see the sky, and the sweat rusheth to my face even as in the time of summer.' Then said Isis unto Râ, 'O tell me thy name, holy father, for whosoever shall be delivered by thy name shall live.' [And Râ said], 'I have made the heavens and the earth, I have ordered the mountains, I have created all that is above them, I have made the water, I have made to come into being the great and wide sea, I have made the "Bull of his mother," from whom spring the delights of love. I have made the heavens, I have stretched out the two horizons like a curtain, and I have placed the soul of the gods within them. I am he who, if he openeth his eyes, doth make the light, and, if he closeth them, darkness cometh into being. At his command the Nile riseth, and the gods know not his name. I have made the hours, I have created the days, I bring forward the festivals of the year, I create the Nile-flood. I make the fire of life, and I provide food in the houses. I am Khepera in the morning, I am Râ at noon, and I am Imu at even.' Meanwhile the poison was not taken away from his body, but it pierced deeper, and the great god could no longer walk.

Then said Isis unto Râ, 'What thou hast said is not thy name. O tell it unto me, and the poison shall depart; for he shall live whose name shall be revealed.' Now the poison burned like fire, and it was fiercer than the flame and the furnace, and the majesty of the god said, 'I consent that Isis shall search into me, and that my name shall pass from me into her.' Then the god hid himself from the gods, and his place in the boat of millions of years was empty. And when the time arrived for the heart of Râ to come forth, Isis spake unto her son Horuss, saying, 'The god hath bound himself by an oath to deliver up his two eyes' (i.e. the sun and moon). Thus was the name of the great god taken from him, and Isis, the lady of enchantments, said, 'Depart poison, go forth from Râ. O eye of Horus, go forth from the god, and shine outside his mouth. It is I who work, it is I who make to fall down upon the earth the vanquished poison; for the name of the great god hath been taken away from him. May Rd live, and may the poison die, may the prison die, and may Râ live!' These are the words of Isis, the great goddess, the queen of the gods, who knew Râ by his own name.

But after he was healed, the strong rule of the old sun-god had lost its vigour, and even mankind became hostile against him: they became angry and began a rebellion.

The power of the divine Name is shown in many another old tradition. Effective as were the qualities ascribed to magic knots, amulets, drugs, and the great body of mystic rites connected with their use, as also to conjuring by numbers, incantations, and so forth, in that great home of magic, Chaldea, all these yielded to the power of the god's name. Before that everything in heaven, earth, and the underworld bowed, while it enthralled the gods themselves. In the legend of the descent of Ishtar to the underworld, when the infernal goddess Allat takes her captive, the gods make vain effort to deliver her, and in their despair beg Hea to break the spell that holds her fast. Then Héa forms the figure of a man, who presents himself at the door of Hades, and awing Allat with the names of the mighty gods, still keeping the great name secret, Ishtar is delivered.

Lane says that it is a Moslem belief that the prophets and apostles to whom alone is committed the secret of the Most Great Name of God (El-Izm-el-Aazam) can by pronouncing it transport themselves (as on Solomon's magic carpet, spun for him by the jinn) from place to place at will, can kill the living, raise the dead, and work other miracles. By virtue of this name, which was engraved on his seal-ring, Solomon, or Suleyman, subjected the birds and the winds, and, with one exception, all the jinn, whom he compelled to help in the building of the Temple at Jerusalem. By pronouncing it, his minister Asaf was transported in a moment to the royal presence. Sakhr was the genie who remained unsubdued, and one day when the Wise King, taking a bath, intrusted the wonderful ring to one of his paramours, the demon assumed Solomon's form, and, securing possession of the magic jewel, usurped the throne, while the king, whose appearance was forthwith changed to that of a beggar, became a wanderer in his own realm. After long years the ring was found in the stomach of a fish, Sakhr having thrown it away on his detection, and so Solomon 'came to his own again. In the *Toldoth Jeshu*, a pseudo-life of Jesus of Jewish compilation, there are two legends concerning the Unutterable Name. One relates that this name was engraved on the corner-stone of the

Temple. 'For when King David dug the foundations he found there a stone on which the Name of God was graven, and he took it and placed it in the Holy of Holies. But as the wise men feared lest some ignorant youth should learn the name and be able to destroy the world--which God avert!--they made by magic two brazen lions, which they set before the entrance of the Holy of Holies, one on the right, the other on the left. Now, if any one were to go within and learn the holy Name, then the lions would begin to roar as he came out, so that from alarm and bewilderment he would lose his presence of mind and forget the Name.

'Now Jeshu left Upper Galilee and came secretly to Jerusalem, and he went into the Temple, and learned there the holy writing; and after he had written the incommunicable Name on parchment he uttered it, with intent that he might feel no pain, and then he cut into his flesh and hid the parchment with its inscription thereon. Then he uttered the Name once more, and made so that his flesh healed up again. And when he went out at the door the lions roared, and he forgot the Name. Therefore he hasted outside the town, cut into his flesh, took the writing out, and when he had studied the signs he retained the Name in his memory.'

The second legend, which tells of an aerial conflict between Jeshu and Judas before Queen Helena (!), says that 'when Jeshu had spoken the incommunicable Name, there came a wind and raised him between heaven and earth. Thereupon Judas spake the same Name, and the wind raised him also between heaven and earth. And they flew, both of them, around in the regions of the air, and all who saw it marvelled. Judas then spake again the Name, and seized Jeshu and sought to cast him to the earth. But Jeshu also spake the Name, and sought to cast Judas down, and they strove one with the other.' Ultimately Judas prevails, and casts Jeshu to the ground, and the elders seize him; his power leaves him; and he is subjected to the tauntings of his captors. Being rescued by his disciples, he hastened to the Jordan; and when he had washed therein his power returned, and with the Name he again wrought his former miracles.

As has been remarked already, belief in the power of the Name would lead to hesitation in the use of it, lest evil fall on him who uttered it, and, since some term would be necessary, to coinage of substitutionary names. To the Mohammedans, Allah is but an epithet in place of the Most Great Name to whose wonder-working power reference has been made. The three great gods of the limitless Hindu pantheon, Brahmâ, Vishnu, and Siva, have as their symbol the mystic OM or Aims, the repetition of which is believed to be all-efficacious in giving knowledge of the Supreme. Leviticus xxiv. 16, 'He that blasphemeth the name of the Lord, he shall surely be put to death, and all the congregation shall certainly stone him: as well the stranger, as he that is born in the land, when Ii blasphemeth the name of the Lord, shall be put to death,' is sometimes cited as the warrant for the avoidance of the 'holy and reverend name Yahweh, or Jehovah; but perhaps it influence of Oriental metaphysics on the Jew coupled with the persistence of barbaric ides about names, may have led to a substitution which appears to have been post-exilian. 'Adona and 'Elohim' are sometimes used in the place Yahweh, but more often the god is anonymous 'the name' being the phrase adopted. A doubtful tradition says that 'Jehovah' was uttered but once a year by the high priest on the Da of Atonement when he entered the Holy of Holies, and, according to Maimonides, it was spoken for the last time by Simon the Just. The real name of Confucius is so sacred that is a statutable offence to pronounce it. Commissioner Yeh, in a conversation with M: Wingrove Cooke, said, 'Tien means properly only the "material heaven," but it also means Shang-te, "supreme ruler," "God"; for as it is not lawful to use His name lightly, we name Him by His dwelling-place, which is in Tien.' In his references to Osiris, Herodotus remarks in one place, where he speaks of the exposure of the sacred cow, 'At the season when the Egyptians beat themselves in honour of one of their gods whose name I am unwilling to mention in connection with such a matter'; and in another, 'On this lake it is that the Egyptians represent by night his sufferings whose name I refrain from mentioning.'

The Father of History here gives expression to a feeling dominant throughout every stage of culture. He differs no whit from that typical savage, the Australian black-fellow, into whose ear, on his initiation, the elders of the tribe whisper the secret name of the sky-god--Tharamulün, or Daramulun,--a name which he dare not utter lest the wrath of the deity descend upon him.

THERE is no essential difference between Names of Power and Words of Power, and the justification of any division lies wholly in its convenience. For although the implication may be that the one is associated with persons, and the other with things, we have sufficing evidence of the hopeless entanglement of the two in the barbaric mind. Both are regarded as effective for weal or woe through the magic power assumed to inhere in the names, and through the control obtained over them through knowledge of those names. In examining this attitude, it may be well to bear in mind what has been said already concerning magic as a primitive form of science; bad science, it is true, yet possessing the saving grace of some perception of possible relations between phenomena. For here the apparatus of the priest--prayer, sacrifice, and so forth--is superseded, or, at least, suspended, in favour of the apparatus of the sorcerer with his 'whole bag of tricks '-- spells, incantations, curses, passwords, charms, and other machinery of white or black magic. In his invaluable Asiatic Studies, Sir Alfred Lyall remarks that among the lower religions 'there seem always to have been some faint sparks of doubt as to the efficacy of prayer and offerings, and thus as to the limits within which deities can or will interpose in human affairs, combined with embryonic conceptions of the possible capacity of man to control or guide Nature by knowledge and use of her ways, or with some primeval touch of that feeling which now rejects supernatural interference in the order and sequence of physical processes. Side by side with that universal conviction which ascribed to divine volition all effects that could not be accounted for by the simplest experience, and which called them miracles, omens, or signs of the gods, there has always been a remote manifestation of that less submissive spirit which locates within man himself the power of influencing things, and which works vaguely toward the dependence of man on his own faculties for regulating his material surroundings.

Words of Power, broadly classified, may be divided, with more or less unavoidable overlapping, into (a) Creative Words; (b) Mantrams and their kin; (c) Passwords; (d) Spells or Invocations for conjuring up the spirit of the dead, or for exorcising demons, or for removing spells on the living; and (e) Cure-Charms in formulae or magic words. Of each of these five intermingled classes a few examples will suffice.

(a) CREATIVE WORDS

The confusion of person and thing meets us at starting, and the deification of speech itself warrants its inclusion in this section. Probably the most striking example of such deification is the Hindu goddess Vãc, who is spoken of in the Rig Veda as 'the greatest of all deities; the Queen, the first of all those worthy of worship,' and in one of the Brahmanas, or sacerdotal commentaries on the Vedas, as the 'mother ' of those sacred books. Another hymn to her declares that when she was first sent forth, all that was hidden, all that was best and highest, became disclosed through love. By sacrifice Speech was thought out and found, and he who sacrifices to her 'becomes strong by speech, and speech turns unto him, and he makes speech subject unto himself.' When Vãc declares--

'Whom I love I make mighty, I make him a Brãhman, a Seer, and Wise. .

I have revealed the heavens to its inmost depths, I dwell in the waters and in sea,
Over all I stand, reaching by my mystic power to the height beyond.
I also breathe out like the wind, I first of all living things.
Beyond the heavens and this earth I have come to this great power,'

echoes of the sublime claims of Wisdom in the Book of Proverbs haunt the ear.

'The Lord possessed me in the beginning of his way before his works of old.
I was set up from everlasting, from the beginning, ever the earth was.
When there were no depths, I was brought forth; when there were no fountains abounding with water.
Then I was by him, as one brought up with him: am was daily his delight.'

In the Wisdom of Solomon, the high place of 'Chockmah' or Wisdom, as co-worker with the Deity, is still more prominent; in the Targums 'Memra' or 'Word' is one of the phrases substituted by the Jews for the great Name; while the several speculations concerning the nature and functions of Wisdom in the canonical and apocryphal books took orderly shape in t:he *Logos*, the Incarnate Word of God, of Saint John's Gospel. In Buddhism, *Manjusri* is the personification of Wisdom,although in this connection we have to remark that this religion has no theory of the origin of things, and that for the nearest approach to the *Vãc* of Hinduism (as the possible influence of which on the wisdom the Book of Proverbs, and through it on Logos, nothing can be said here) we must cross into ancient Persia, in whose sacred books we read of Honovar or *Ahuna-variya*, the 'Creating Word' or the 'Word Creator.' When Zarathushtra (Zoroaster) asks Ahuramazda, the Good God of the Parsi religion, which was the word that he spoke 'before the heavens, the water, the earth, and so forth,' Ahuramazda answers by dwelling on the sacred Honovar, the mispronunciation of which subjects a man to dire penalties, while 'whoever in this my world supplied with creatures takes off in muttering a part of the Ahuna-variya, either a half, or a third, or a fourth, or a fifth of it, his soul will I, who am Ahuramazda, separate from paradise to such a distance in width and breadth as the earth is.' In his translation of *Salaman and Absal*, wherein these lines occur,

'. . . The Sage began,
O last new vintage of the vine of life
Planted in Paradise; O Master-stroke,

And all-concluding flourish of the Pen,
KUN-FA-YAKUTN,

Edward FitzGerald appends as note on Kun-fa-Yakun, 'Be, and it is--the famous word of Creation stolen from Genesis by the Kurán.' In that book we read, 'The Originator of the heavens and the earth when He decrees a matter He doth but say, unto it, "BE," and it is,' --a declaration which the Genesis creation-legend, doubtless a transcript of Accadian originals, anticipates in the statement, 'And Elohim said, Let there be light, and there was light.' In this connection the three shouts of the Welsh, which created all things, should be noted.

(b) MANTRAMS

Dr. Wallis Budge remarks that among the magic formulae of which the ancient Egyptians made use for the purpose of effecting results outside man's normal power, was repetition of the names of gods and supernatural beings, certain ceremonies accompanying the same. For they believed that every word spoken under given circumstances must be followed by some effect good or bad. The same idea prompts the belief of the Irish peasant that a curse once uttered must alight on something; it will float in the air seven years, and may descend any moment on the party it was aimed at Allied to this is the old Scandinavian belief that a curse is powerful unless it can be turned back, when it will harm its utterer, for harm some one it must. The origin of the Egyptian superstition lies further back than Dr. Budge suggests, although he is probably correct in assuming that its development received impetus from the belief that the world and all things therein came into being immediately after Thoth, the god of writing, especially of sacred literature, had interpreted in words the will of the Deity in respect of the creation, and that creation was the result of the god's command.

Belief in the virtue of mystic phrases, faith in whose efficacy would seem to be increased in the degree that the utterers do not know their meaning, is world-wide. The old lady who found spiritual 'comfort in 'that blessed word, Mesopotamia,' has her representatives in both hemispheres, in the *matamanik* of the Red Indian and the *karakias* of the New Zealander, while the Roman Catholic can double the number of beads on his rosary by exchanging strings with the Tibetan. The latter, as we know, fills his 'praying-wheels,' more correctly, praising-wheels, with charms or texts from his sacred books, the words of wonder-working power frequently placed therein, or emblazoned on silk flags, being 'Om Mani padme hum,' 'Ah, the jewel in the lotus,' i.e. 'the self-creative force is in the kosmos.'

But most typical of all are the sacred formulas of the Hindus, the *mantrams* which are believed 'to enchain the power of the gods themselves.' They are charged with both bane and bliss; there is nothing that can resist their effect. At their bidding the demons will enter a man or be cast out of him, and the only test of their efficacy is supplied by themselves, since a stronger *mantram* can neutralise a weaker. 'The most famous and the most efficacious mantrani for taking away sins, whose power is so great that the very gods tremble at it, is that which is called the *gayatri*. It is so ancient that the Vedas themselves were born from it Only a Brahmin has the right to recite it, and he must prepare himself by the most profound meditation. It is a prayer in honour of the sun. There are several other *mantrams* which are called *gayatri*, but this is the one most often used.' Next in importance to the *gayatri*, the most powerful *mantram*, is the monosyllable OM or AUM, to which reference has been made. But, all the world over, that which may have been the outcome of genuine aims has become the tool of necromancers, soothsayers, and their kin. These recite the mystic charms for the ostensible purpose of fortune-telling, of discovering stolen property, hidden treasure, and of miracle-mongering generally. Certain *mantrams* are credited with special power in the hands of those who have the key to the true pronunciation, reminding us of the race--test in the pronunciation of the old word *Shibboleth*. To the rishis or sorcerers who know how to use and apply these *bija-aksharas*, as such *mantrams* are called, nothing is impossible. Dubois quotes the following story in proof of this from the Hindu poem, *Brahmottara-Kanda*, composed in honour of Siva:--'Dasarha, King of Madura, having married Kalavali, daughter of the King of Benares, was warned by the princess on their wedding-day that he must not exercise his rights as a husband, because the *mantram of the five letters* which she had learned had so purified her that no man could touch her save at the risk of his life, unless he had been himself cleansed from all defilement by the same word-charm. The princess, being his wife, could not teach him the *mantram*, because by so doing she would become his guru, and, consequently, his superior. So the next day both husband and wife went in quest of the great Rishi, or penitent Garga, who, learning the object of their visit, bade them fast one day and bathe the following day in the holy Ganges. This being done, they returned to the Rishi, who made the husband sit down on the ground facing the East, and, having seated himself by his side, but with face to the West, whispered these two words in his ear, "Namah Sivaya." Scarcely had Dasarha heard these marvellous words before a flight of crows was seen issuing from different parts of his body, these birds being the sins which he had committed.'

That the *mantrams* do not now work the startling effects of which tradition tells, is explained by the Brahmins as due to mankind now living in the Kali-Yuga, or Fourth Age of the World, a veritable age of Iron; but they maintain that it is still not uncommon for miracles to be wrought akin to that just narrated, and to this which follows. Siva had taught a little bastard boy the mysteries of the *bjja-akshara* or *mantram* of the five letters. The boy was the son of a Brahmin widow, and the stain on his birth had caused his exclusion from a wedding-feast to which others of his caste had been invited. He took revenge by pronouncing two or three of the mystic letters through a crack in the door of the room where the guests were assembled. Immediately all the dishes that were prepared for the feast were turned into frogs. Consternation spread among the guests, all being sure that the mischief was due to the little bastard, so, fearing that worse might happen, they rushed with one accord to invite him to come in. As he entered, they asked his pardon for the slight, whereupon he pronounced the same words backwards, and the cakes and other refreshments appeared, while the frogs vanished. 'I will leave it,' remarks the Abbé, 'to some one else to find, if he can, anything amongst the numberless obscurations of the human mind that can equal the extravagance of this story, which a Hindu would nevertheless believe implicitly.' Were that veracious recorder of Oriental belief and custom alive, he would be supplied from the narratives of proceedings at spiritualist séances with examples of modern credulity as strong as those which he collected in the land on which the Mahatmas look down from their inaccessible peaks.

(c) PASSWORDS

The famous Word of Power, 'Open, Sesame,' pales before the passwords given in the *Book of the Dead*, or, more correctly, *The Chapters of Coming Forth by Day*. This oldest of sacred literature, venerable four thousand years B.C., contains the hymns, prayers, and magic phrases to be used by Osiris (the common name given to the immortal counterpart of the mummy) in his journey to Amenti, the underworld that led to the Fields of the Blessed. To secure unhindered passage thither, the deceased must know the secret and mystical names of the Gods of the Northern and Southern Heaven, of the Horizons, and of the Empyreal Gate. 'As the Egyptian made his future world a counterpart of the Egypt which he knew and loved, and gave to it heavenly counterparts of all the sacred cities thereof, he must have conceived the existence of a waterway like the Nile, whereon he might sail and perform his desired voyage.' Strangest evidence of the Egyptian extension of belief in Words of Power is furnished in the requirement made of the deceased that he shall tell the names of every portion of the boat in which he desires to cross the great river flowing to the underworld. Although there is a stately impressiveness throughout the whole chapter, the citation of one or two sentences must suffice. Every part of the boat challenges the Osiris:--

'Tell me my name,' saith the Rudder. 'Leg of Hapiu is thy name.'

'Tell me my name,' saith the Rope. 'Hair, with which Anubis finisheth the work of my embalmment, is thy name.'

'Tell us our names,' say the Oar-rests. 'Pillars of the underworld is your name.'

And so on; hold, mast, sail, blocks, paddles, bows, keel, and hull each putting the same question, the sailor, the wind, the river, and the river-banks chiming in, and the Rubric ending with the assurance to the deceased that if 'this chapter be known by him,' he shall 'come forth into Sekhet-Aarru, and bread, wine, and cakes shall be given him at the altar of the great god, and fields, and an estate . . . and his body shall be like unto the bodies of the gods.'

But the difficulties of the journey are not ended, because ere he can enter the Hall of the Two Truths, that is, of Truth and Justice, where the god Osiris and the forty-two judges of the dead are seated, and where the declaration of the deceased, that he has committed none of the forty-two sins, is tested by weighing his heart in the scales against the symbol of truth, Anubis requires him to tell the names of every part of the doors, the bolts, lintels, sockets, woodwork, threshold, and posts; while the floor forbids him to tread on it until it knows the names of the two feet wherewith he would walk upon it. These correctly given, the doorkeeper challenges him, and, that guardian satisfied, Osiris bids the deceased approach and partake of 'the sepulchral meal.' Then after more name-tests are applied, those of the watchers and heralds of the seven ants or mansions, and of the twenty-one pylons of the domains of Osiris, the deceased 'shall be among those who follow Osiris triumphant. The gates of the underworld shall be opened unto him, and a homestead shall be given unto him, and the followers of Horus who reap therein shall proclaim his name as one of the gods who are therein.'

(d) SPELLS AND AMULETS

In the famous scene in *Macbeth*, when the witches make the 'hellbroth boil and bubble' in their 'caldron,' Shakespeare drew upon the folk-lore of his time. Two years before he came to London, Reginald Scot had published his *Discoverie of Witchcraft*, a work which, in Mr. Lecky's words, 'unmasked the imposture and delusion of the system with a boldness that no previous writer had approached, and an ability which few subsequent writers have equalled.' In that book may be found the record of many a strange prescription, of which other dramatists of Shakespeare's period, notably Middleton, Heywood, and Shadwell, made use in their thaumaturgic machinery. Scot's exposure of the 'impietie of inchanters' and the 'knaverie of conjurers' is accompanied by examples of a number of spells for raising the various grades of spirits, from the ghost of a suicide to the innumerable company of demons. In each case the effectiveness of the spell depends on the utterance of names which are a jumble of strange or manufactured tongues. For example, the spirits of the 'Airy Region' are conjured by 'his strong and mighty Name, Jehovah,' and by his 'holy Name, Tetragrammaton,' and by all his 'wonderful Names and Attributes, Sadat, Ollon, Emillat, Athanatos, Paracletus.' Then the exorcist, turning to the four quarters, calls the names, 'Gerson, Anek, Nephrion, Basannah, Cabon,' whereupon the summoned spirits, casting off their phantasms, will stand before him in human form to do his bidding, to bestow the gift of invisibility, foreknowledge of the weather, knowledge of the raising and allaying of storms, and of the language of birds. Then the exorcist dismisses them to their aerial home, in 'the Name of the Father, Son, and Holy Ghost.

The witch of Endor secured the appearance of Samuel by the mere invocation of his name, a far simpler process than availed the medieval necromancer, for he had to go to the grave at midnight with candle, crystal, and hazel wand on which the Name of God was written, and then, repeating the words, 'Tetragrammaton, Adonai, Agla, Crabon,' to strike on the ground three times with his wand, thereby conjuring the spirit into the crystal.

The importance which the ancient Egyptians attached to dreams is well known. It was the universal belief that they were sent by the gods; and as matters of moment hinged on them, magic was brought into play to secure the desired dream. Among the formulae used for this purpose which survive is the following:--Take a cat, black all over, which has been killed: prepare a tablet, and write these words with a solution of myrrh, also the dream desired, which put in the mouth of the cat:--' Keimi, Keimi, I am the Great One, in whose mouth rests Mommon, Thoth, Nanumbre, Karikha .... the sacred Lanieê ien aëo eieeieiei aoeeo,' and so on in a string of meaningless syllables which were supposed to convey the hidden name of the god, and thereby make him subject to the magician. Then, as the conclusion, 'Hear me, for I shall speak the great Name, Thoth. Thy name answers to the seven vowels.'

The Babylonian libraries have yielded a large number of incantations for use against evil spirits, sorcery, and human ills generally, the force of the magic conjurations being increased in the degree that they are unintelligible. For it is needful to preserve the old form of the name, because, although the meaning may be lost, another name, or a variation of it, would not possess the same virtue.

Although

'The lion and the lizard keep
The courts where Jamshyd gloried and drank deep,'

these references to the superstitions that dominated the ancient civilisations of the East, and through them, in their elaborated magical forms, of the West, are of service to-day. That they persisted so long is no matter of wonder, when we remember how late in human history is perception of the orderly sequence of phenomena; and that persistence also explains why like confusion prevails in communities where the scientific stage has not been reached. In this matter, even in these post-Darwinian days, 'there are few that be saved' from the feeling that, in some vaguely defined way, man can influence the unseen by the power of spoken words. The terrible curses which accompanied the once-dreaded excommunication have their pale echoes in our Commination Service (which to most persons nowadays only suggests the 'Jackdaw of Rheims'), and both are the outcome of the barbaric belief that the utterance of the word has a direct effect on the man against whom it is spoken. The belief in that power was extended to the written word. Reginald Scot gives the following charm 'against thieves,' which 'must never be said, but carried about one':--'I doo go, and I doo come unto you with the love of God, with the humility of Christ, with the holmes of our blessed ladle, with the faith of *Abraham*, with the justice of *Isaac* with the vertue of David, with the might of *Peter*, with the constancie of *Paule*, with the word of God, with the authoritie of *Gregorie* with the praier of *Clement*, with the floud Jordan, pppcgegaqq est pti ka bglk 2 ax tgtb am g 242 i q; pxcgkqqaqqpqqr. Oh onelie Father + oh onlie lord + and Jesus + passing through the middest of them + went + In the Name of the Father + and of the Sonne + and of the Holie ghost

   To this class belong Gnostic amulets with the~ cabalistic inscriptions; the Jewish phylacteries or frontlets, whose virtue was supposed to rest in the texts shut up in the leathern case; amulets with the secret name of God chased on then worn by those very barbaric Christians, the Abyssinians, to avert the evil eye and ward off, demons; passages from the Koran enclosed in bags and hung on Turkish and Arab horses to protect them from like maleficence; and prayers to the Madonna slipped into charm-cases an worn by the Neapolitans. Horns, as symbolic of the lunar cusps, are a common form of amulet against the evil eye, whether 'overlooking' man or beast, and the superstitious Italians believe that, in default of a horn or some horn-shape object, the mere utterance of the word *corno coma* is an effective talisman. Mr. Elworthy tells of a fright which he unwittingly gave secondhand bookseller in Venice when asking about a copy of Valletto's *Cicalata sul Fascino*. On hearing the last two words of the title, 'the man actually turned and bolted into his inner room, leaving the customer in full possession the entire stock.' In modern Greece garlic the popular antidote to the evil eye, so the term σκόρδον is used to undo the effect of any hast or inauspicious words. The German peasant says *unberufen* ('unspoken' or 'called back'), and raps three times under the table if any word 'tempting Providence' has fallen from his lips many a fragment of cabalistic writing is cherished and concealed about their persons by the rustics of Western Europe as safeguards against black magic; and not a few still resort, in times of devotional book at random, hoping to see in the passage that first catches the eye direction as to action, or some monition of the future. For this purpose the ancients consulted the Iliad or the Aeneid; but, changing only the instrument while retaining the belief, *Sortes Homericae* and *Sortes Virgilinae* have been superseded by *Sortes Biblicae*. As for the spells which guard the departed, the *Book of the Dead* supplied any number. Its chapters were inscribed on basalt scarabs to protect the Osiris in his passage to Amenti; on heart-shaped amulets, so that the heart of the man might not be stolen from his tomb; while on others his name was engraved, because the blotting-out of a man's name brought with it his extinction. There is nothing new under the sun. At the burial of the late Czar a prayer was chanted, and also printed on a scroll of paper, and then placed by the priest in the hands of the corpse as a document enabling him, when wandering about the spirit-world during the first few days after death, to pass on his way unmolested by evil spirits.

(e) CURE-CHARMS

As gods of healing, both Apollo and Aesculapius were surnamed Paean, after the physician to the Olympian deities, and the songs which celebrate the healing power of Apollo were also called by that name. Ever in song have the deeper emotions found relief and highest expression, while the words themselves have been credited with magic healing power. The earliest fragment in the Book of Genesis is the song in which Lamech chants the 'slaying of a man to his wounding'; and as the word charm (Lat. carmen, a song) itself indicates, the old incantations were cast in metrical form. Songs are the salve of wounds. When Odysseus was maimed by the boar's tusk, his kinsfolk sang a song of healing; and when Wäinamöinen, the hero-minstrel of the Kalevala, cut his knee in hewing the wood for the magic boat, he could heal the wound only by learning the mystic words that chant the secret of the birth of iron, while he could finish the stern and forecastle only by descending to Tuoni (the Finnish underworld) to learn the 'three lost words of the master.' The same old hero, when challenged to trial of song by the boastful youngster Joukahainen, plunges him deep in morass by the power of his enchantment, and releases him only on his promising to give him his sister Aino in marriage. In his Art of Poesie, written three centuries ago, Puttenham quaintly says that poetry 'is more ancient than the artificiall of the Greeks and Latines, coming by instinct of nature, and used by the savage and uncivill, who were before all science and civiltie. This is proved by certificate of merchants and travellers . . . affirming that the American, the Perusine, and the very canniball, do sing, and also say, their highest and holiest matters in certain riming versicles.' Hence the part which 'dropping into poetry' plays in saga, jâtaka, and folk-tale, little snatches of rhyme lending effect and emphasis to incident, and also aid to memory, as in our title-story-

'Nimmy nimmy not,
My name's Tom Tit Tot.'

Italian folk-medicine, which perhaps more than in any other country in Europe has preserved its empirical remedies, whose efficacy largely depends on magic formulae being uttered over them, has its inconsequential jingle-charms. Traces of the use of these occur among the polished Romans; while Grimm refers to a song-charm for sprains which was current for a thousand years over Germany, Scandinavia, and Scotland. How the pre-Christian cure-charms are transferred by change of proper names to the Christian,

like the conversion of Pagan deities into Christian saints, is seen in these original and Christianised versions:--

'Phol and Woden
went to the wood;
then was of Balder's colt
his foot wrenched;
heald
then Sinthgunt charm'd it,
and Sunna her sister;
then Frua charm'd it, row,
and Volla her sister;
flesh;
then I'Voden charm'd it,
as he well could,
as well the bone-wrench,
as the blood-wrench,
as the joint-wrench;
bone to bone,
blood to blood,
joint to joint,
as if they were glued together.'

'Jesus rode to the heath,
There he rode the leg
of his colt in two,
Jesus dismounted and

it;
Jesus laid marrow to mar-

Bone to bone, flesh to

Jesus laid thereon a leaf,
That it might remain
in the same place.'

Probably a like substitution of names disguises many barbaric word-spells; for medicine remained longer in the empirical stage than any other science, while the repute of the miracles of healing wrought by Jesus largely explains the invocation of his name over both drug and patient. The persistence of the superstition is seen in a story told, among others of the like character, in Miss Burne's *Shropshire Folk-Lore*. A blacksmith's wife, who had suffered from toothache, was given a charm by a young man who told her to wear it in her stays. As so as she had done so the pain left her, and never troubled her again. It was 'words from Scripture that cured her,' she, said, adding that she had relieved 'a many with it.' After some trouble she consented to make a copy of the talisman. It proved to be an imperfect version of an old ague charm given in Brand, and this the form in which the woman had it: 'In the Name of God, when Juses saw the Cross wich he was to be crucfied all is bones began to shiver. Peter standing by said, Jesus Christ cure all Deseces, Jesue Christ cure thy tooth ak The following is a copy of a charm also against toothache, stitched inside their clothing and worn by the Lancashire peasants: 'Ass Saint Petter sat at the geats of Jerusalm our Bless Lord and Sevour Jesus Crist Pased by ai Sead, What Eleth thee? Hee sead, Lord, my teeth ecketh. Hee sead, Arise and follow mee and thy teeth shall never Eake Eney mour. Fiat + Fiat + Fiat.' Among cures for the same complaint in Jewish folk-medicine one prescribes the driving of a nail into the wall, the formula, 'Adar Gar Vedar Gar' being uttered, and then followed by these words: 'Even as this nail is firm in the wall and is not felt, so let the teeth of So-and-so, son of So-and-so, be firm in his mouth, and give him no pain.' In North-German charm-cures the three maidens (perchance echoes of the Norns) who dwell in green or hollow ways gathering herbs and flowers to drive away diseases may re-appear in the disguise to which we are accustomed in the angels of many a familiar incantation, as in this for scalds or burns--

'There were three angels came from East and West--
One brought fire and another brought frost,
And the third it was the Holy Ghost,
Out fire, in frost, in the Name of the Father, Son, and Holy Ghost.'

Brand gives a long list of saints whose names are invoked against special diseases, and the efficacy believed to attach to the names of Joseph and Mary is shown by sending children suffering from whooping-cough to a house where the master and mistress are so named. 'The child must ask, or rather demand, bread and butter. Joseph must cut the bread, Mary must spread the butter and give the slice to the child, then a cure will certainly follow. In Cheshire it is unlucky to take plain currant-cake from a woman who has married a man of her own-name--a superstition allied to the belief in ill-luck resulting from marriage between people whose surnames begin with the same letter--

'If you change the name and not the letter,
You change for the worse and not for the better.'

In the preparation of a drink for the frenzied, the Saxon leech recommended, besides recitations of litanies and the paternoster, that over the herbs twelve masses should be sung in honour of the twelve apostles, while the name of the sick should be spoken when certain simples are pulled up for his use. So, among the Amazulu, the sorcerer Ufaku called Uncapayi by name that the medicine might take due effect on him, A medieval remedy for removing grit from the eye was to chant the psalm 'Qui habitat' three times over water, with which the eye was then to be douched, while modern Welsh folk-lore tells of the farmer who, having a cow sick on a Sunday, gave her physic, and then, fearing that she was dying, ran into the house to fetch a Bible and read a chapter to her. An Abyssinian remedy for fever is to drench the patient daily with cold water for a week, and to read the Gospel of Saint John to him; and in the Chinese tale of the Talking Pupils, Fang is cured of blindness by a man reading the Kuang-ming sutra to him. Among the Hindus, doctors would be regarded as very ignorant, and would inspire no confidence, if they were unable to recite the special *mantram* that suits each complaint, because the cure is attributed quite as much to the *mantram* as to the treatment. It is because the European doctors recite neither *mantrams* nor prayers that the native puts little faith in their medicines. Midwives are called *Mantradaris* because the repeating of *mantrams* by them is held to be of great moment at the birth of the child. 'Both the new-born babe and its mother are regarded as specially liable to the influence of the evil eye, the inauspicious combination of unlucky planets or unlucky days, and a thousand other baleful elements. And a good midwife, well primed with efficacious *mantrams*, foresees all these dangers, and averts them by reciting the proper words at the proper moment.' Obviously, it is but a step from listening to the charm-working words of sacred texts to swallowing them; hence the Chinese practice of burning papers on which charms are written and mixing the ashes with tea; and the Moslem practice of washing off a verse of the Koran and drinking the water. The amulet written on virgin parchment, and suspended towards the sun on threads spun by a virgin named Mary, equates itself with the well-known cabalistic Abracadabra charm against fevers and agues, which was worn for nine days, and then thrown backwards before sunrise into a stream running eastward.

It has been remarked already that among all barbaric peoples disease and death are believed to be the work of evil spirits, either of their own direct malice prepense or through tile agency of sorcerers. 'Man after man dies in the same way, but it never occurs to the savage that there is one constant and explicable cause to account for all cases. Instead of that, he regards each successive death as an event wholly by itself--apparently unexpected--and only to be explained by some supernatural agency.' In West Africa, if a person dies without shedding blood it is looked on as uncanny. Miss Mary Kingsley tells of a woman who dropped down dead on a factory beach at Corisco Bay. 'The natives could not make it out at all. They were irritated about her conduct. "She no sick; she no complain; she no nothing, and then she go die one time." The *post-mortem* showed a burst aneurism. The native verdict was, 'She done witch herself,'--*i.e.* she was a witch eaten by her own familiar. That verdict was logical enough, as logical as that delivered by English juries two centuries ago under which women were hanged as witches. In trying two widows for witchcraft at Bury St. Edmunds in 1664, Sir Matthew Hale, a humane and able judge, lak it down in his charge 'that there are such creatures as witches I make no doubt at all the Scripture affirms it, and the wisdom of all nations has provided laws against such persons. Given a belief in spirits, the evidence of their direct or indirect activity appears in aught that is unusual, or which has sufficing explanation ii the theory of demoniacal activity. In barbarian belief, the soul or intelligent principle in which a man lives, moves, and has his being plays all sorts of pranks in his normal life, quitting the body at sleep or in swoons, thereby giving employment to an army of witch-doctors in setting traps to capture it for a ruinous fee Consequently, all the abnormal things that happen are attributed to the wilfulness of alien spirits that enter the man and do the mischief The phenomena attending diseases lend further support to the theory. When any one is seen twisting and writhing in agony which wring piercing shrieks from him, or when he shiver and shakes with ague, or is flung to the ground in convulsive fit, or runs 'amok' with incoherent ravings, and with wild light flashing from his eyes, the logical explanation is that a disease-demon has entered and 'possessed' him. Man is the same everywhere at bottom; if there are many varieties, there is but one species. His civilisation is the rare topmost shoot of the tree whose roots are in the earth, and whose trunk and larger branches are in savagery. Hence, although the study of anatomy and physiology--in other words, of structure and function--paved the way, no real advance in pathology was possible until the fundamental unity and interdependence of mind and body were made clear, the recency of which demonstration explains the persistency of barbaric theories of disease in civilised societies. The Dacotah medicine-man reciting charms over the patient and singing, 'He-la-li-ah' to the music of beads rattling inside a gourd, is the precursor of the Chaldean with his incantations to drive away the 'wicked demon who seizes the body, or the wind spirit whose hot breath brings fever,' and to cure 'the disease of the forehead which proceeds from the infernal regions.' The drinking of holy water and herb decoctions out of a church-bell, to the saying of masses, so that the demon might be exorcised from the possessed, has warrant in the legends which tell of the casting-out of 'devils' by Jesus and, through the invocation of his Name, by the apostles; while the continuity of barbaric ideas in their grosser form has illustration in the practice of a modern brotherhood in the Church of England--the Society of St. Osmund-- based on the theory that not only unclean swine, but the sweet flowers themselves, are the habitat of evil spirits. In the *Services of Holy Week from the Sarum Missal* the 'Clerks' are directed to 'venerate the Cross, with feet unshod,' and to perform other ceremonies which are preceded by the driving of the devil out of flowers through the following 'power of the word':

'I exorcise thee, creature of flowers or branches: in the Name of God+the Father Almighty, and in the Name of Jesus Christ+ His son, our Lord, and in the power of the+Holy Ghost; and henceforth let all strength of the adversary, all the host of the devil, every power of the enemy, every assault of fiends, be expelled and utterly driven away from this creature of flowers or branches.' Here the flowers and leaves *shall be sprinkled* with HOLY WATER, and *censed* (pp. 3-5).

The antiquity of the demon-theory of disease has curious illustration in the prehistoric and long surviving practice of trepanning skulls so that the disease-bringing spirit might escape. Doubtless the disorders arising from brain-pressure, diseased bone, convulsions, and so forth, led to the application of a remedy which, in the improved form of a cylindrical saw, and other mechanism composing the trephine, modern surgery has not disdained to use where removal of a portion of the skull or brain is found necessary to afford relief. Prehistoric trepanning, as evidenced by the skulls found in dolmens, caves, and other burying-places all the world over, from the Isle of Bute to Peru, was effected by flint scrapers, and fragments of the skulls of the dead who had been thus operated upon were cut off to be used as amulets by the living, or placed inside the skulls themselves as charms against the dead being further vexed. The trepannings in Michigan, about which we have more complete details, were always made after death, and only on adults of the male sex. They were probably obtained by means of a polished stone drill, which was turned round rapidly. Whether, or in what degree, the Neolithic surgeon supplemented his rude scalpel by the noisy incantations which are part of the universal stock-in-trade of the savage medicine-man, we shall never know; but the practice of his representatives warrants the inference which connects him with the mantram-reciters, the charm-singers, and all others who to this day believe that the Word of Power is the most essential ingredient in the remedy applied.

THE NAME AND THE SOUL

AT the close of this survey of evidence that, in barbaric psychology, the name is believed to be an integral part of a man, the question which suggests itself is, *What part?*

The importance attached by the ancient Egyptians to the name in connection with its owner's personality has been already referred to. They had no doubt whatever that if the name was blotted out, the man ceased to exist. In their composite and conglomerate theories of the individual we have refinements of distinction which surpass anything known in cognate barbaric ideas. The Hidatsa Indians believe that every human being has four souls which at death depart one after the other. But this is simplicity itself compared to Egyptian ontology. In this we find (1) the *sahn*, or spiritual body; then (2) the *ka*, or double (other-self), which, although its normal dwelling-place was the tomb, could wander at will, and even take up its abode in the statue of a man. It could eat and drink, and, if the sweet savour of incense and other ethereal offerings failed, could content itself with feeding on the viands painted on the walls of the tomb. Then there was (3) the *ba*, or soul, about which the texts reveal opposing views, but which is usually depicted as a bird with human heads and hands. To this follow (4) the *ab*, or heart, held to be the source both of life and of good and evil in the life, and, as the seat of vital power, without which there could be no resurrection of the body, jealously guarded against abstraction by the placing of heart-shaped amulets on the mummy. Next in order is (5) the *khaibit* or shadow; then (6) the *khu* or shining covering of the spiritual body which dwelt in heaven with the gods; and (7) the *sekhem* or personified power of the man.

Last, but not least, was (8) the REN or name that 'part of the immortal Ego, without which no being could exist.' Extraordinary precautions were. taken to prevent the extinction of the *ren* and in the pyramid texts we find the deceased making supplication that it may flourish 'germinate' along with the names of the gods. The basal connection between this practice and that of the importance attached to the record the name in the 'Lamb's Book of Life' as ensuing admission to heaven, which is a canon popular modern belief, is too obvious for comment. Among the Pacific races, Bancroft tells us, 'the name assumes a personality, it is the shadow spirit or other-self of the flesh-and-blood person. Civilised and savage are at one in their identification of the soul with something intangible, breath, shadow, reflection, flame, and so forth. But it is the cessation of breathing which, the long-run, came to be noted as the never failing accompaniment of death; and where the condensation of the exhaled breath is visible, there would be support lent to the theory of souls as gaseous or ethereal. In every language, from that of the barbaric Aino to classic Greek and modern English, the word for 'spirit' and for 'breath' is the same. Hence, the unsubstantial 'name' falls into line with the general nebulous conception of spirit, and, were barbaric languages less mutable, it might be possible to find some help to an equation between 'name' and 'soul' in them. But as even seemingly stable things like numerals and personal pronouns undergo rapid change among the lower races, 'two or three generations sufficing to alter the whole aspect of their dialects among the wild and unintelligent tribes of Siberia, Africa, and Siam,' the search is hopeless. Some light, however, is thrown upon the matter by languages in which favourable circumstances have preserved traces of family likeness and of mutations. In asking the question, whether there be any evidence from philology to show what part of a man his name is supposed to be, Professor Rhys has been first in the field to supply materials for an answer. He says that 'as regards the Aryan nations, we seem to have a clue in an interesting group of words from which I select the following: Irish *ainm*, "a name," plural *anmann*; Old Welsh *anu*, now *enw*, also a name; Old Bulgarian *ime*; Old Russian *emnes*, *emmens*, accusative *emnan*, and Armenian *anwan*--all meaning "a name." To these some scholars would add, and rightly, I think, the English word name itself, the Latin *nomen*, Sanskrit *naman*, and the Greek όνομα; but, as some others find a difficulty in thus grouping these last-mentioned words, I abstain from laying any stress on them. In fact, I have every reason to be satisfied with the wide extent of the Aryan world covered by the other instances which I have enumerated as Celtic, Prussian, Bulgarian, and Armenian. Now, such is the similarity between Welsh *enw*, "name," and *enaid*, "soul," that I cannot help referring the two words to one and the same origin, especially when I see the same or rather greater similarity illustrated by the Irish words *ainm*, "name," and *anim*, "soul."

This similarity between the Irish words so pervades the declension of them, that a beginner frequently falls into the error of confounding them as medieval texts. Take, for instance the genitive singular *anma*, which may mean either "animae" or "nominis"; the nominative plural *anmanna*, which may be either "animae or "nomina"; and *anmann*, either "animarum or "nominum," as the dative *anmannaib* may like-wise be either "animabus" or "nominibus." In fact, one is tempted to suppose that the partis differentiation of the Irish forms was only brought about under the influence of Latin with its distinct forms of *anima* and *nomen*. Be that as it may, the direct teaching of the Celtic vocables is that they are all to be referred to the same origin in the Aryan word for breath or breathing, which is represented by such words as Latin *anima*, Welsh *anadl*, "breath," and Gothic *anan*, "blow" or "breathe," whence the compound preterite *uz*-on twice used in the fifteenth chapter of St. Mark's Gospel to render εξέπνευσε, "gave up the ghost." Lastly, the lesson which the words in question contain for the student of man is that the Celts, and certain other widely separated Aryans, unless we should rather say the whole Aryan family, believed at one time not only that the name was a part of the man, but that it was that part of him which is termed the soul, the breath of life, or whatever you may choose to define it as being.

The important bearing of this evidence from language on all that has preceded is too clear to need enlarged comment. It adds another item to the teeming mass of facts witnessing to the psychical as well as the physical unity of man. It has become a truism that at the same intellectual level, however wide the zones that separate him, he explains the same phenomena in much the same way; any set of facts gathered in one quarter being complementary to any set of facts gathered in another quarter.

One by one the theories armed with assumption of the presence of caprice and elements of disorder in the universe have been defeated until they reached their last stand in the citadel of Mansoul. From that final retreat they are being ousted, because man's extension of the methods of inquiry into his surroundings to his inner nature makes clear that he is no exception amongst animated beings, but has his place in the universal order.

Printed in Great Britain
by Amazon